Prescription: Romance™

"What is going on, Fee?

"You bite his head off when you see him and now you're cross because he's gone. Anyone would think you're in love with the man."

"That's ridiculous!" Fiona was outraged by the suggestion. She glared at her sister. "I've got to go."

"It wasn't so ridiculous the last time he was here, was it? Or did you think I hadn't noticed?"

"That was a long time ago, Laura. Ancient history—forget it."

"I had, actually—until tonight. The question is, have you?"

Alison Roberts was born in New Zealand and, she says, "lived in London and Washington, D.C., as a child and began my working career as a primary school teacher. A lifelong interest in medicine was fostered by my doctor and nurse parents, sharing a flat with doctors and physiotherapists on leaving home and marriage to a housesurgeon, who is now a consultant cardiologist. I have also worked as cardiology technician and research assistant. My husband's medical career took us to Glasgow for two years—an ideal place and time to start my writing career. I now live in Christchurch, New Zealand, with my husband, daughter and various pets."

Prescription: Romance™

A Chance in a Million

Alison Roberts

HARLEQUIN®

TORONTO • NEW YORK • LONDON
AMSTERDAM • PARIS • SYDNEY • HAMBURG
STOCKHOLM • ATHENS • TOKYO • MILAN • MADRID
PRAGUE • WARSAW • BUDAPEST • AUCKLAND

ISBN 0-373-63119-7

A CHANCE IN A MILLION

First North American Publication 1999.

This edition published by arrangement with Harlequin Books S.A.

Visit us at www.romance.net

Printed in U.S.A.

CHAPTER ONE

'ARE you OK?'

'Mmm. Fine.' Fiona Donaldson depressed the foot control to release a quantity of soap onto her hands, wiping them together briskly before reaching for the small scrubbing-brush.

'Why do you ask?'

'You seem very quiet this morning.'

'Most people are quiet at seven-thirty a.m.' Fiona scrubbed busily between her fingers, around her nails and then began on her forearms. 'Besides, you know me. I'm the deeply thoughtful, philosophical type, not given to idle banter in the OR scrub room.'

Martin Cox laughed. He dried his own hands carefully on the sterile towel and watched his junior colleague as she rinsed off the lather. Fiona's long fingers had the natural grace of a ballet dancer as she held her hands down, letting the water run from wrist to fingertips, then angling them up, rinsing from wrists to elbows. Turning off the tap with a nudge from her elbow, Fiona glanced up at Martin.

'Perhaps I'm nervous. My first shot at a major op with you breathing down my neck. Most people would be a wreck.'

'Not you. I doubt very much if you've ever suffered an attack of nerves in your life. You were itching to take over the first time you assisted me.' He regarded the obstetric and gynaecology department's most junior registrar thoughtfully. 'You probably would have done a great job, too.'

'Thanks.' Fiona plunged her arms into the gown being held out for her by the scrub nurse, and then turned to have the back tied.

'You're not really nervous, are you?' Martin snapped his glove-cuff over the sleeve of his gown.

'No. It should be a straightforward hysterectomy. And I've got the cavalry ready to thunder in, if needed.' The hazel eyes crinkled at the corners as Fiona smiled at her senior registrar.

'So, what's the problem, then? Could it be that you're regretting refusing the date I offered you last week?'

Fiona laughed at that and shook her head as she pulled the fingers of her gloves into place.

'Something's up,' persisted Martin. 'You've just had a weekend down home and I'm not being regaled with stories about the birthing complications of sheep, successes at the dog trials or the escapades of the latest horse you're breaking in.'

'It's not lambing season, and my dogs and horses obey my every whim.' Fiona held her hands up clear of her gown as she moved purposefully towards the swing doors.

'I can believe that.' Martin Cox's gaze was openly admiring above his mask as he followed Fiona into the theatre.

'You're doing a superb job,' he commented some time later. 'Put another clamp on the lateral fornix of the vagina and then you can divide and detach the cervix.'

Personal interchange had been forgotten, due to

Fiona's intense concentration on her task. The uterus and ovaries having been removed, the young doctor turned her attention to tying off and using diathermy to close the previously clamped blood vessels. It was not until the final layers of suturing were in place that she relaxed slightly and noticed how stiff her neck had become. Martin watched as the patient was transferred to a trolley.

'That should cure her dysfunctional bleeding problems. Congratulations, Fiona. I couldn't have done it better myself.'

'Thanks, Martin. I enjoyed it.' Fiona stripped off her gloves and dropped them into the bin.

'Good. You can do the next one as well, then. Just a diagnostic D and C. I'll do the investigative laparoscopy after her.'

'Is that it for this morning?' Fiona's gown went into the soiled linen bag and she moved back to the basins to begin scrubbing again.

'No way. We've got a prolapse to repair and another D and C—this time for an incomplete abortion. Then we get to meet the new boss and have some lunch, if we're lucky.' Martin paused in his scrubbing and eyed Fiona thoughtfully.

'That's what's bothering you, isn't it? You're afraid I'm going to tell him about your sloppy work, poor punctuality and dreadful attitude to the job.'

They both laughed, but Fiona bit her lip beneath the mask as she dried her hands. If anything was enough to bother her, this upcoming meeting certainly was. She had been stewing about it ever since the departmental meeting last month, when her consultant, Jack Owens, had announced he would be away for three months.

'As you know,' Jack Owens had begun, 'my wife's family is based in Wales, and for some time we have wanted to take the children on an extended visit. The opportunity has arisen quite by chance.'

'Amazing what happens over a couple of beers at these conferences,' Martin Cox had quipped.

Jack Owens had grinned. 'Quite. I happened to be talking to a colleague about our intention to actively pursue the advances in the field of diagnostic and operative laparoscopy, and expressed my desire for advanced training. They're in the forefront with new procedures and, I'm delighted to say, were prepared to take me on.'

'What's happening about cover here?' A consultant from another Obs and Gynae firm had looked openly worried at the thought of the extra workload to be distributed.

'That's the best part—as far as management here is concerned,' Jack had replied. 'One of their consultants, already an expert in the field, is prepared to come here and take my position as an exchange visit. Mr Jonathan Fletcher is a New Zealander but has been at the Cardiff Royal Infirmary for the last four years, and he...'

But Jack Owens's words had flowed over Fiona unheard.

Jonathan Fletcher. Jon. Even the name had provoked an emotional response that quickened her breath and heartbeat. The dream that had refused to evaporate completely had surfaced with painful clarity. Perhaps it was true that she'd never had the right to such a dream, but it had been the biggest part of her life for almost as long as she could remember. The sense of betrayal she had felt at being seemingly dismissed from his life had certainly been real enough. Even more than six years had failed to mute it sufficiently to be forgettable.

Now, thanks to the ambitions of her present boss, Jonathan Fletcher was about to reappear in her life and Fiona found herself in turmoil. Forcing herself to concentrate on her surroundings, she found that Jack Owens was winding up his briefing.

'And management has set up a working party to act on his recommendations as far as new equipment and such goes.'

'That's fantastic!' The enthusiastic response of Martin Cox was echoed by the other consultants.

'With the new equipment and the training he can provide, we'll be more than ready for you when you get back.'

'Exactly.' Jack Owens nodded. 'It's a superbly satisfactory arrangement all round.'

Fiona was not sure she agreed. She found she had to clear her throat to make her voice audible.

'Is he bringing his family with him?'

Jack looked taken aback. 'I've no idea. I'm ashamed to say I don't even know if he's married.'

Oh, he is. Fiona's words were unspoken but her expression was enough for Jack Owens to give her a quizzical look.

'Do you know Jon Fletcher, Fiona?' Her hesitation spared her having to answer as Martin broke in. 'The three-month time-frame—is that definite?'

'Not necessarily,' Jack replied. 'There's the possibility of extension. We'll see how it goes on both sides.' He stood up to indicate the close of the meeting. 'From reports I've had, you should find Jon a worthwhile colleague. I hope you'll make him welcome.'

Was it coincidence that had made him direct his final comment at her, Fiona wondered, or could he sense how difficult it was going to be for her to even work with the guest consultant, much less make him feel welcome?

'It's a speculum.' Martin Cox spoke with feigned patience. 'You put it in—'

'I know,' Fiona muttered. She took the instrument from Martin. 'Sorry. I was miles away.'

Silently Fiona damned Jonathan Fletcher and the effect he had on her concentration, before dismissing him completely from her thoughts and turning to the task in hand. It was a procedure in which she now felt thoroughly confident, but that was no excuse for her lapse.

If Martin Cox would settle for the friendship she would gladly offer Fiona could tell him why she was behaving out of character, but Martin had made it clear he would like a lot more than friendship. He was only one of the willing candidates who had appeared since Fiona entered medical school, but she had never been tempted to offer more than friendship.

She told herself it was devotion to study and then commitment to her career, but she knew if she analysed the reason she would find it had a lot to do with the fact that the crushing disappointment she had felt five years ago on learning about Jon's marriage had never been entirely suppressed. And he had been such an impossible yardstick for anyone else to measure up to.

The rest of the busy morning list worked well as a distraction, and Fiona stretched luxuriously after stripping off her gown and gloves for the last time. Pulling her mask down, she reached up to remove her hat. Martin paused in stripping off his own gloves.

'I do love seeing a girl let her hair down.'

Fiona shook her head. 'It feels good, I must say. The weight is a real pain after a morning like this. Maybe I should get rid of it.'

Martin eyed the waist-length braid of russet hair. 'I hope you never do,' he said sincerely. 'How did you learn to do that fancy plaiting?'

Fiona laughed. 'It's French plaiting. Basically the same as getting a horse's tail ready for showing, which is how I learned. Of course, it's a bit trickier doing it behind one's own head.'

In fact, her arms had ached with the effort, and Fiona had berated herself for doing anything that could be interpreted as preparation for the coming meeting. But that hadn't stopped her feeling pleased with the result, or taking the extra few minutes to apply mascara to the thick tangle of lashes that framed her hazel eyes and foundation to cover the freckles that always seemed too obvious on her pale skin.

The introduction to their new boss was scheduled to take place in the office of one of the other Obs and Gynae consultants, Philip Reece. Fiona arranged to meet Martin outside the office in ten minutes and made a dash for the showers. While it was quite usual for Fiona Donaldson to be seen still in theatre gear when busy around the wards, she had decided it was entirely inappropriate on this occasion.

The recent sleepless night had given Fiona ample time to prepare for this encounter. Excitement, trepidation and anger had vied for the emotional upper hand. She had countered the onslaught by planning down to the last detail exactly what she would wear, say and, hopefully, feel.

'Professional. That's the key,' she had decided. The emotional disturbance was unproductive and pointless. What was past was past. This encounter was a test for her maturity and she was going to pass with flying colours, as usual.

Fiona was not a devotee of fashion, although her slim figure and height of five feet ten would have made her a perfect clothes horse. Most happily comfortable wearing jodhpurs or jeans, she compromised for work by wearing leggings with stylish but definitely casual tops. She now tended to avoid reprimands, unspoken or otherwise, by spending much of her day wearing the shapeless but acceptable theatre gear, throwing her white coat over the top for duties on the ward.

Fiona owned two skirts: one serviceable and uninspiring, which made frequent appearances for outpatient clinics, the other having been bought to attend a friend's wedding last year. Made of soft wool fabric, which clung to her slim hips then flared to mid-calf length, it was a dark shade of rust that toned perfectly with her hair. It was this skirt that Fiona reached for as she finished dressing, tucking a white silk blouse into the waistband.

A glance into the mirror as she shrugged on her white coat satisfied Fiona that she looked every inch the professional. She straightened her shoulders and raised her chin. She was ready.

Martin Cox whistled softly at Fiona's approach, but the compliment was ignored. Over his shoulder, through the open door of the office, she could see

Philip Reece. He was in earnest conversation with their guest consultant—Jonathan Fletcher.

Fiona stopped abruptly, alarmed at the impact on her emotions seeing him had. It was like a physical blow and she had to catch her breath. The registrars' arrival in the corridor had gone unnoticed and the conversation continued. Philip Reece was frowning unhappily.

'It will be a big disappointment to the department if you don't wish to take over Jack's supervision of the IVF unit. You've got such a wealth of experience in the field.'

'Too much experience, I'm afraid,' Jonathan Fletcher was also frowning. 'I gave up that area a couple of years ago. I'm probably well out of date by now.'

'I doubt that very much.' Philip smiled as he shook his head. 'Think about it, anyway, but there's absolutely no pressure. We can easily cover that area ourselves. Now, tell me...?—'

Fiona's senses, initially stunned, began to work overtime as they soaked in what she could see and hear of the man in the office. The passing of time was obvious, and on first impression had given him a maturity and air of sophistication that was startling. Jonathan had always seemed vaguely uncomfortable with his height of six feet four inches, and the thinness that had accompanied it had made for a slightly awkward image.

Now his chest and shoulders had broadened, and his posture suggested he enjoyed his height advantage. Even more astonishing, he was wearing his dark, wavy hair long, neatly scraped back and fastened into a short ponytail at the back. It gave him an exotic,

European look that Fiona knew would raise more than a few eyebrows in this conservative neck of the medical woods.

Then Fiona noticed the streaks of silver, so obvious in the tiny curls which had escaped taming at his temples. Jonathan's serious expression also accentuated the new lines around his eyes, and he looked much older than his thirty-two years.

Despite the confidence he exuded, Fiona had the impression of an aura of sadness about him, and it reminded her strongly of the first time she had met him. For a split second she wanted to move forward and touch him, to convey comfort and to forgive his desertion. Her desire for contact was rudely dispelled, and as quickly forgotten, by a nudge from Martin's elbow.

'Who's getting married?' he whispered. 'Did I miss my invitation?'

Fiona frowned. Martin's banter had not been part of her calculations in the professional appearance.

'It's the skirt.' Martin grinned. 'It only comes out for weddings, doesn't it? Just give me the word and I can dash out and hire a morning suit.'

Fiona laughed. She did like Martin, and his mischievous grin was hard to resist. He had never made any secret of his admiration, and his attempts at wooing her, along with her good-humoured rebuffs, had become part of the ward routine. They both knew he was not really serious any more.

The peal of Fiona's laughter made Philip glance up. The consultant smiled with real pleasure.

'Ah, Jon. Let me introduce your senior registrar, Martin Cox, and the youngest but by no means the least significant member of your team—Dr Fiona

Donaldson.' He drew Fiona forward by her elbow. 'Fiona—I'd like you to meet Jonathan Fletcher.'

But the introduction was clearly superfluous. Jon had reached out and taken hold of both Fiona's hands.

'Penny! It can't be!'

Fiona couldn't help but be gratified at the warmth of the grip on her hands, and the way delight lit up those dark grey eyes and then spread, washing any hint of sadness from the finely featured face. Then the anger that had been bubbling for the last few weeks surfaced. How dared Jonathan assume he could just step back into her life and expect her to welcome him? She tried unsuccessfully to pull her hands free.

'You two have obviously met before.' Philip was watching the interchange with great interest.

'What's with the "Penny" business?' Martin was also watching closely.

'It was a family nickname,' Fiona explained tightly, 'on account of my hair.'

'The colour of a newly minted penny,' Jon murmured. He still hadn't taken his eyes off Fiona's face.

'It was a long time ago,' Fiona added. Her tone was crisp. 'Ancient history.' With a determined yank, she withdrew her hands from Jonathan's and had the satisfaction of seeing a disconcerted frown pass over his face.

'Yeah. I can see you've rusted a bit.' Martin was now looking distinctly put out by the unexpected reunion.

Jonathan glanced up at the senior registrar's tone and his gaze flicked from Martin to Fiona. He grinned at Martin.

'Penny—Fiona, I mean—is like my kid sister. We

go way back. I went through med school with her brother, Daniel.'

'Oh.' Martin visibly relaxed. 'Why on earth didn't you say anything, Fiona?'

Fiona's irritation at Martin's possessiveness was fanned by the resentment she felt at being referred to as a 'kid sister'. She didn't believe Jonathan had been blind enough to miss knowing how she had really felt. In fact, she knew he hadn't. And now he was making an assumption regarding her relationship with Martin. Fiona took a deep breath. What did it matter what Jonathan Fletcher thought? He was no longer a part of her life.

'We haven't been in touch.' Fiona's tone was icy. 'I wasn't sure Jonathan would even remember me.'

Her words clearly struck home, but Fiona was the only one to recognise the flash of pain in Jon's expression. It was replaced instantly by the quirky one-sided grin she remembered so well as a plea for forgiveness—or friendship. But the grin was directed at her senior colleagues.

'The last time I saw Pen—Fiona, she was galloping up a long hill, bareback, yelling like a mad cowboy and rounding up several hundred sheep single-handed.'

Philip laughed. 'She tackles a ward round in a similar manner. It can be most entertaining.'

Fiona gave an exasperated sigh. This was hardly going to impress Jonathan as to her professional abilities or maturity. She wanted to end the conversation about herself, and couldn't resist taking a stab at the affectionate manner in which Jonathan was reminiscing.

'Perhaps it was only single-handed because the assistance I had was totally inadequate.'

Jonathan laughed, ignoring the dismissive tone. 'You didn't really expect me to ride that bucking bronco without a saddle, did you?'

Fiona was spared having to answer by Philip's interruption.

'You two obviously have a lot to catch up on. Would you like to postpone the rest of the tour, Jon?'

Fiona knew that Jonathan was trying to catch her eye and she turned her gaze to her watch with relief.

'I have an antenatal ultrasound clinic starting in five minutes.' So much for lunch, she added silently.

'And I'd better get started on the rest of the antenatals,' Martin concurred. 'Delighted to meet you, Mr Fletcher. Welcome to Christchurch.'

Jonathan shook the extended hand. 'Thanks. And call me Jon. I look forward to working with you. Both.'

Fiona knew he had held out his hand to her as she turned to follow Martin. She also knew she was being extremely rude in not echoing the words of welcome or even saying goodbye. To hell with it, she decided as she silently followed Martin towards outpatients. She really couldn't care what he thought of her. It was only for three months, after all. Even if Mr Jonathan Fletcher's visit was extended she was due to change runs at that point so the problem would be solved. One way or another.

CHAPTER TWO

'I'M JUST measuring the circumference of the baby's head, now, Cheryl.' Fiona moved the last calliper point on the screen and then pushed another button. She reached for a pen to record the measurement. 'We add that to some other measurements and it gives us a pretty accurate idea of the baby's weight and growth rate.'

Fiona moved the ultrasound transducer over the oiled surface of Cheryl Batten's well-rounded abdomen. She glanced down to her left where a small girl was seated on a high stool.

'Shall we see if we can find something more interesting to put on the TV now?'

The toddler nodded. 'I want Big Bird.'

Fiona and her patient laughed. The sound covered the noise of the door closing, and the three occupants of the small, darkened room were too focused on their task to see the tall figure of Jonathan Fletcher lean quietly against the corner wall.

'Don't think I can manage Big Bird, but how about this?' Fiona pointed to the screen. 'There's baby's arm and hand. Look, it's moving. I think baby's waving at you.'

The child laughed gleefully and waved back at the monitor.

'I think that's all we need to do now, Cheryl.' Fiona returned the mother's smile. 'Any questions?'

'Can you...? Do you know what sex the baby is?'

Fiona grinned. 'Are you sure you want to know?'

Mrs Batten nodded nervously. 'Jim, my husband, is so sure it's going to be a boy. I don't mind either way, but if it isn't maybe I could sort of prepare him.'

Fiona moved the transducer in a slow circuit of the abdomen and then began angling it with care.

'I suppose he's already got some rugby boots ready?'

Cheryl Batten sounded embarrassed. 'I've managed to hold him back so far.'

'There.' Fiona spoke with satisfaction. 'Can you see?'

'Is that—? It's a boy, isn't it?'

'Sure is. Better send Jim out shopping.' Fiona wiped Mrs Batten's skin with a soft towel. 'Now, if you'd like to get dressed, they should be about ready for you in the antenatal clinic.' She turned back to the child.

'You're going to have a little brother, Gemma. Isn't that great?'

Gemma looked doubtful. 'Can I see Big Bird now?'

Fiona was startled to find Jon in the room as she turned to usher her patient out—startled and more than a little annoyed at being observed unknowingly. The fright and the anger that followed had to be the only reason her heart tripped and the flush warmed her cheeks, she decided. She pointed Mrs Batten in the right direction and then turned back to the ultrasound room.

'How long have you been there?'

'Long enough.' Jon gave his one-sided grin. 'Sorry. I didn't want to interrupt you.' His grin broadened to both sides. 'And I was hoping to catch a glimpse of

Big Bird.' He watched Fiona roll the attachment at the end of the bed to spread a clean layer of paper over the mattress. 'You like kids, don't you?'

'Of course. Don't you?' Fiona's glance was brief and her tone cool. 'I imagine you've got a few of your own by now.'

The silence that greeted her remark made her look up again. Jonathan's gaze was direct but wary, and there was something else in his expression. An unspoken apology, perhaps?

'No,' he said quietly. 'No kids.'

'All in good time, I suppose.' Fiona tried to sound cheerful. 'Now, if you'll excuse me, I left Mrs Jensen filling up her bladder. She's probably ready to explode by now.'

'Penny. We have to talk.' Jon's hand caught Fiona's wrist. 'Mrs Jensen's bladder will cope, I promise.'

'Not long enough to rectify nearly six years of total non-communication.' Fiona's anger surfaced. 'And why bother?' she snapped. 'You've obviously got your own life now and we've never been allowed to be part of it.' She pulled her wrist away. 'Excuse me. If I run late with the ultrasounds it will hold up the whole antenatal clinic.'

Mrs Jensen's bladder was admirably full and Fiona was glad of the basic task of a first ultrasound check. The patient's husband was also present, and Fiona allowed herself to catch the excitement of the glimpse of their first child. She spent longer than was strictly necessary on the examination and then had to push to get through the rest of the busy clinic, but that suited her very well. It stopped her mind straying back too frequently to the encounter with Jon.

Her resentment was increasing with each contact. The confident charm and friendliness Jonathan displayed would make him a popular member of staff instantly, Fiona conceded, especially in conjunction with his physical attractiveness. But he had no right to expect her to welcome him back into her life. She didn't want any part of Jonathan Fletcher.

With the clinic over, Fiona headed purposefully back towards the ward. After her first solo hysterectomy she was more than usually interested in how the patient was progressing.

Entering the ward office to get the nursing notes for Mrs Wilson, Fiona found them in the hands of Martin Cox. Martin was talking to Jonathan. They both looked up as Fiona approached.

'Don't fret,' Martin said with a smile. 'We're not about to put her on the critically ill list.'

'She's doing very well,' added Jon. 'I understand congratulations are in order.'

'Thanks.' Fiona dropped her gaze. 'I guess I won't disturb Mrs Wilson again if you've just checked on her.'

There was a moment of awkward silence, then Jon cleared his throat 'I gather we're on call tomorrow and it gets pretty busy around here. I'd appreciate all the help you can give me with the standard protocols and so forth.'

'You've got it.' Martin dropped Mrs Wilson's chart on the trolley and nudged Fiona. 'We're a great team, eh?'

'Mmm.' Fiona didn't want any increase in Jon's assumptions regarding her relationship with the senior registrar. Then she softened her cool response with a smile. 'I guess we are pretty good.'

Martin busied himself, writing up a report on a patient he had just seen, and Fiona found another awkward silence as Jonathan seemed to be waiting for her to speak. His gaze was curious but a smile lurked close to the surface. Clearly no offence had been taken at her earlier rudeness, and Fiona was irritated by his confidence. She decided to ignore the silence, unhooking the stethoscope from around her neck and folding it to stuff into the pocket of her white coat.

'It's late,' she announced. 'I'm off home for some dinner.'

'Lentil soup,' Martin muttered. 'Yum.' He shot a glance at Jonathan. 'Fiona's vegetarian, you know.'

'No, I didn't know,' Jonathan responded easily. 'I guess there are a few changes I wouldn't know about.'

'You're not wrong there.' Fiona shrugged off her white coat and draped it carelessly over her arm.

'Perhaps I'll find out what they are.' The lopsided grin was charming, the tone conciliatory.

Fiona returned the smile tightly. 'I wouldn't bet on it.'

Fiona dumped her load of books and carry-bags onto the huge desk in her living room, and quickly crouched to return the enthusiastic greeting of the sleek black and white dog at her feet. A champion Border collie in her day, Belle had pined on the farm when Fiona left and she had recently decided to try having her in the city. It was an arrangement that now suited them both.

Belle was old enough to appreciate the long, quiet days of luxury, and Fiona was often thankful for the company. The heavy head on her foot as she studied, the warm weight against her leg when she slept, stopped the small cottage being oppressively lonely, and Belle still had enough energy to relish the weekend jaunts or, better still, a few days back home on the farm.

Fiona exchanged her skirt for a faded pair of denim jeans but tucked in the ends of the same silk shirt. She lit the small gas fire, flicked on some lamps and then transferred the bulging grocery bags into her tiny kitchen.

'I'm going to cook something special for dinner,' she told Belle. 'It's been a rough day.'

Fiona busied herself in the kitchen, enjoying the distraction of cooking. Adding crushed garlic to the sauted onion, she poured herself a glass of wine and took a large swallow. By the time she'd added the sliced courgettes and mushrooms to the pan Fiona was feeling much more relaxed, the tensions of the day almost forgotten. She planned to curl up with a book while she ate her dinner.

Belle's warning bark, followed by the loud knock at her door, shattered the relaxed atmosphere. Cursing quietly, Fiona turned down the heat under the pan and wiped her hands on a towel. Opening the door, she found Jonathan Fletcher leaning against the verandah post. Like herself, he was wearing faded blue jeans, and the rugged navy fisherman's rib jersey was just like the type he'd used to wear on the farm. He was holding a large bunch of flowers and a bottle of wine.

'You shouldn't open the door to just anyone, you know,' he said seriously.

'Obviously not,' Fiona agreed, unsmiling. She watched Belle retreat to the kitchen, having decided her mistress was not in danger. 'How did you get my address?'

'I used my considerable charm on someone in management.' Jonathan flashed Fiona a quick grin and she couldn't help returning it—briefly.

'I can imagine,' she said dryly.

Jonathan held out the flowers and wine. 'I came to make peace,' he said quietly. 'We do have to work with each other for a while.'

Fiona sighed. 'That's true.'

'It would be a lot more pleasant if we could be friends again.'

Fiona tilted her head to one side. 'I suppose so,' she said reluctantly. 'OK. I apologise for being rude to you and thank you—these are lovely.' She took the bunch of yellow and white chrysanthemums, acutely aware of her fingers brushing against his as she did so. She began to close the door.

'That doesn't smell like lentil soup,' Jonathan commented.

'Oh, help—dinner!' Fiona turned and fled back to the kitchen, just in time to prevent the vegetables scorching. She moved the pan and looked up to find Jonathan had followed her. He was still holding the bottle of wine.

'I knew you were on the point of inviting me in,' he said winningly. 'And, besides, you forgot this.' He waved the bottle. 'Good grief!' Jonathan put the bottle down with a thump. 'That can't be Belle!'

The dog's eyes opened at the sound of her name. 'Do you remember me, girl?' Jonathan asked softly. 'I helped Pen train you when you were a puppy.'

Belle's tail thumped in agreement, and Fiona watched as Jonathan stooped to stroke the sleek head.

She hadn't been on the point of inviting him into her home—anything but—and she now struggled with the urge to ask him to leave. But there was no way she could bring herself to interrupt the intense atmosphere as Jonathan petted Belle. After a long minute he looked up, and Fiona was troubled by the depth of sadness in his expression.

'I'd forgotten the feeling of a family. A home...' His voice trailed off.

Fiona spoke briskly to cover her own emotion. Feeling sorry for Jonathan Fletcher had definitely not been on her agenda.

'It's not much of a home. One bedroom, a living room, kitchen and bathroom. But it's close to the hospital and suits the two of us. We go down to the farm whenever we can.'

'The two of you?' Jonathan's quick glance over his shoulder as he rose made Fiona laugh.

'Belle and me. Did you think I had a husband stashed away?'

'I wouldn't put it past you.'

'That reminds me.' Fiona reached for her glass and took a large gulp of wine. 'Your wife—Clare, isn't it? Where have you stashed her?'

There was a long silence. Then Jonathan spoke calmly. 'I'm on my own, Penny. I've been on my own for a long time. My divorce came through three years ago.' He pointed to Fiona's glass. 'Do you think I might have one of those?'

Fiona hesitated for a long moment, then nodded slowly. She was disconcerted by the news. Not that it made any difference to the way she felt—it just didn't fit with the image she had created for him. Leaving Jonathan to fill his own glass, Fiona added enough fettucine for two to the pot of boiling water on the stove.

'I guess I'd better feed you,' she said lightly. 'Poor lost soul that you are.'

'You sound like your mum.' Jonathan smiled. 'I like that.' He sat on the edge of the kitchen table, sipping his wine and watching her.

Fiona was silent, seemingly intent on cutting thick slices from a loaf of fragrant herb bread. Surely he couldn't know that was exactly what her mother had once called him?

Jonathan Fletcher had been a contemporary of Fiona's much older brother, Daniel. He had first come to the Donaldson family's high country sheep station as an employee—the vital holiday job he'd needed to support himself through medical school. He had rapidly become more than an employee, however. At first reluctant to join the family group for anything more than meals, there had been a guarded wariness about the young man that had frightened the youngest member of the Donaldson clan.

Fiona had been eleven at the time, a tall, skinny child with bright copper hair and too many freckles. She had heard her mother describe the stranger sadly as 'a lost soul', but by the time she was old enough to understand the reference the description was no longer appropriate. Jonathan Fletcher had responded in a very short time to the warm welcome and loving atmosphere of the Donaldson home and had become, over the years, a much-loved family member.

Fiona glanced at Jonathan as she drained the pasta. 'Mum was really worried about you for a long time. She still talks about you every time I'm home,' she said accusingly. 'The last we heard was that

Christmas card, telling us you were getting married, and then—nothing.'

'I know. I'm sorry.' Jonathan refilled their glasses. 'I could come up with all sorts of excuses, but I suppose it's really inexcusable, isn't it?'

'Yes.' Fiona wasn't going to be swayed by explanations.

'You've every right to be angry with me,' Jonathan said slowly. 'But we were friends, weren't we? Good friends?'

Fiona bit her lip. Perhaps that *was* the only perception Jonathan had had of their relationship. Perhaps he had been just too blind to be aware of how she had felt.

Fiona's adoration had been won during that first holiday job on the farm. Jon had sat up with her all night, dribbling eyedroppers full of milk formula into the weak, orphaned lamb she had carried home. The undersized specimen had astounded everyone by becoming the largest ram on the property. Ivan the Terrible, Jon had christened him. He'd become a family pet and a private bond between then. By the time Ivan was being used for stud duties Fiona was fifteen, and desperately in love with Jonathan Fletcher. Memories of boarding school had paled into insignificance compared to the joy of holiday times when they'd all been together again.

Then the fabric had crumbled. After their houseman years Daniel's and Jon's careers had diverged as they'd both sought overseas experience. Daniel had gone to Australia and Jonathan had been thrilled to gain a position in Newcastle, England. Fiona's older sister—Daniel's twin, Laura—married and left home and everything had changed. The fervent promises to stay in touch had apparently been forgotten and the Christmas card, telling the Donaldsons of Jon's marriage, had been the last contact. Her teenage dreams crushed, Fiona had transferred her despair into anger, refusing to admit to sharing her family's deep concern as to his well-being.

'We were, weren't we?' Jonathan's insistent tone broke into Fiona's silence. 'There isn't something I'm missing here? Some sin other than lack of contact that's made you so angry with me?'

Fiona was still silent. What if Jonathan had really not been aware of her feelings, or, worse, had dismissed them as a teenage crush. To confess now would only be to make a fool of herself and give Jonathan an opportunity to rub salt into a wound that Fiona was determined to have—and leave—healed.

'I guess not,' she finally conceded. She wanted to change the subject, and slid a plate of steaming pasta in front of her guest. 'Help yourself to some bread.'

Jonathan picked up his fork but then paused.

'I can't believe you're a doctor. What made you decide on medicine? Last I heard it was going to be law school.'

Fiona laughed wryly. 'Must have had something to do with all those lambs I delivered, I guess. And I kind of missed hearing you and Daniel talk medicine all the time.'

That had been the main reason, though Fiona wasn't about to admit it. A career in medicine had been initially attractive because it had been Jon's career. A part of him, at least, that she could keep.

'Laura got married,' she added quickly. It would be easier if she could keep the conversation away from herself.

'Of course. She was engaged to Alan for as long as I knew her. Are they happy?'

'Oh, yes.' Fiona reached for a slice of bread. 'They've got four kids.'

'What?'

'The first two were twins. They just haven't stopped,' Fiona chuckled. 'They're here in Christchurch, too. Alan's doing a postgraduate agricultural degree, as well as lecturing at the college. They're planning to be back on the farm within a year or two. Dad's not getting any younger and it's a huge property for him to manage.'

'I'd love to see everybody. I'd love to see the farm again.' Jonathan frowned. 'I've often thought about it.'

'Why did you come back, Jonathan?' Fiona asked bluntly. 'After all this time?'

'I'm not sure.' Jonathan looked at Fiona guardedly. 'Maybe it was the pull of nostalgia. Maybe I needed to lay a few ghosts. I certainly wasn't expecting to run into you.'

Fiona raised her glass in mock salute. 'Well, here's to one less ghost to chase, I guess.'

'I didn't mean you—or your family.' Jonathan raised his own glass. 'But I will drink to something.'

'What's that?'

'Friendship. True friendship, that is. Something that a few years of lost contact can't destroy. And…' he touched his glass to Fiona's '…an end to hostilities, perhaps?'

Fiona took a sip of her own wine. 'Perhaps,' she agreed cautiously.

At 7.30 a.m. the next morning Fiona checked in at the labour suite of the the Princess Margaret Hospital.

She was not due on duty until 8 a.m., but she had gained a reputation for being available and well prepared, and was not about to let it slip. Besides, she needed a stiff slug of coffee.

She had remained up for a long time after her guest had left. Their conversation had been carefully impersonal for the rest of the evening, and Fiona had been left feeling that something had been missing. It had taken until 2 a.m. to realise what it was.

Apart from the brief mention of his marriage failure, Jonathan had revealed nothing about himself or his life over the last six years. Was it because she had controlled the conversation to try and keep it away from herself, or did he have something he wanted to hide? Despite herself, and the resentment that still lingered, Fiona felt curious.

She made for the ward kitchen and was amused to find Jonathan Fletcher, stirring sugar into a mug of some rather dark liquid. Perhaps he, too, had been kept awake last night.

'I could do with one of those, seeing as you've found your way around so well.'

Jonathan looked up and smiled. 'Have this one—that is, if you take sugar. It's the least I can do after that delicious meal last night.'

Fiona accepted the mug, nodding at the compliment.

'Where did you learn to cook like that, anyway? I remember the meals on the farm being mostly wonderful roast dinners and sticky puddings.'

'Coronary fodder.' Fiona shook her head. 'We're the enlightened generation.' She gave Jonathan a direct look. 'I've had time to learn a lot of things.'

'So I've noticed.' Jonathan's gaze was intense and

Fiona suddenly felt uncomfortable. She drained her mug quickly, hoping to quell the sudden knot in her stomach.

'Time to head into the salt mines. Martin's covering the gynae side to start with, so I'm staying here.'

'And I've got a consult over at Public to check out.' Jonathan said. 'A young woman with cardiac problems who's pregnant. Could be interesting, but I should be back within an hour. Do the beeps have enough range to work between hospitals?'

Fiona nodded as she rinsed out her mug. 'There's a mobile phone you can take instead though. It's easier than hunting for a phone, especially at traffic lights.'

'Great. Don't hesitate to call if you have any worries. Otherwise, I'll catch up with you later.' Jon paused at the kitchen door and Fiona was aware of the same intense gaze directed at her. She avoided looking up as she rinsed her mug but was finally compelled to do so. Looking as though he was about to say something, but then changing his mind, Jonathan gave her a quick lopsided grin and disappeared through the door.

Fiona shook her head and wondered why she was left with a vague feeling of disappointment.

The team of midwives and nursing staff in the labour suite was excellent and, it was Fiona's favourite place to work. The first admission for the day promised to be enjoyably straightforward. It was the woman's third child and she had waited at home until well into her labour. She was also very clear about what she wanted.

'I hope to do without any pain relief but I wouldn't

mind having gas available. And I want to walk around as much as possible—maybe even deliver standing up. Is that OK?'

'You can do whatever feels right,' said Fiona with a smile, 'though I wouldn't advise hanging upside down from the light fittings. We're just here to help, and take over if anything becomes complicated. Which I don't think it will for you.' She stripped off her gloves. 'The baby's position is great, the heartbeat's strong and you're almost fully dilated already. I'll leave you with Sue, your midwife, but I'll be back to check on you shortly.'

'I want to go home straight afterwards, too.' Anne Smylie groaned as another contraction started and she reached for her husband's hand.

Fiona watched the monitor, at present showing the contraction strength and foetal heartbeat as Anne breathed through the contraction, waiting until it was over before she nodded with satisfaction.

'As long as you stay for a few hours so we can make sure you and the baby are fine there's no reason why you can't go straight home.' Fiona grinned. 'Might be by lunchtime, at this rate.'

'Oh, and no stitches, please.'

'Hmm.' Fiona glanced at the midwife and then back to her patient. 'I see in your notes that you had a bad tear last time. If it looks like happening again we'll do an episiotomy. A small, controlled cut is much easier to repair and heals faster than a large tear. So, less stitches at worst, but we'll hope for the best.' She turned to the midwife. 'Sue, you can take the monitors off and let Anne have her freedom. I'll only be next door if you need me.'

Fiona left her patient walking around her room,

supported by her husband. She didn't anticipate any problems there. In the next room, however, a young woman, Ellen Whitmore, who was having her first baby, was already tiring, having come in late the night before. It was a posterior presentation, and the mother's backache was becoming steadily worse during the long first stage, despite pethidine, and Ellen was becoming distressed.

Fiona was dismayed to find that dilation had not progressed since the last report. Retention of urine was also causing pain, and Fiona organised a catheter before ringing Martin.

'It's an occipito-posterior presentation,' she explained, 'a twenty-two-year-old primigravida. There's no sign of foetal distress yet—heart rate is a steady one forty—but the mother's had just about enough. She's been having contractions every three or four minutes for nearly ten hours and she's still only four, maybe five centimetres dilated. I'm wondering about an epidural and possible acceleration.'

'Contact the anaesthetist and set up an oxytocin infusion, but don't start it just yet. Have a talk to the parents and I'll come down in about ten minutes and have a look at her. Warn her that it may well end up being a forceps delivery. Is Jonathan back yet?'

'Not that I've noticed.'

'Right. I'll just call him before I come down. I've got a case of ovarian cyst torsion, or just possibly an ectopic pregnancy, over here that I think will need to go to Theatre sooner rather than later.'

Fiona put a call out to the duty anaesthetist and wrote the order for the infusion, which she passed to the nursing staff to set up. Having had a talk with Ellen and her husband, she popped back to check on

Anne Smylie. Anne was on her knees, leaning into a large bean-bag. Her husband, John, was rubbing her back and talking quietly. Anne did not notice Fiona's entry and the young registrar glanced enquiringly at the midwife.

'She's well into transition. I'll give you a yell when we need you,' Sue said with a smile. 'I wish all our patients were this easy.'

Fiona silently agreed. On her way back to Ellen's room she was waylaid by another of the midwives, Catherine.

'We've got a problem coming in by ambulance,' she informed Fiona. 'Premature labour in a thirty-eight year-old primigravida. It's a full breech presentation with a query of cephalo-pelvic disproportion, so she was booked for an elective Caesar. She's thirty-five weeks, regular contractions and leaking amniotic fluid.'

'Right. Call me as soon as she arrives. I'll call Mr Fletcher now. I'm not going to tackle that on my own.'

Fiona found that Jonathan was now back in the hospital. Quickly she explained the situation and found his tone reassuring.

'I'll be there by the time she arrives. It's going to take an hour to get this lady of Martin's into Theatre and he should be able to handle it. Do you know where he is at the moment?'

'Yes, here. We're just starting an epidural and oxytocin infusion on a posterior presentation.'

'Tell him that Theatre will be ready for him at eleven forty-five. I'll talk to him again before that.'

'Right.' Fiona excused herself quickly as Sue waved at her. Shaking her head at Martin, who emerged from Ellen's room, she hurried back to her first case. Anne was now half squatting on the bed, a mask held to her face. Fiona quickly scrubbed her hands and donned a pair of gloves and a gown. She noticed Sue had an episiotomy trolley at the ready and she smiled at Anne's nervous-looking husband.

'Just crowned.' Sue smiled cheerfully. 'We've got a terrific team here.'

'OK,' nodded Fiona. She grinned at Anne. 'This is the best part. Try and lie back just a little on the pillows while I see how we're doing.' She added another pillow to the pile and they eased Anne out of her squat.

'Don't push this time,' Fiona ordered as another contraction began and Anne reached for the mask. She slipped a finger past the crowning head to check the cord was not around the baby's neck, at the same time assessing the stretch of perineal tissue to see whether an episiotomy could be avoided.

'No more pushing,' she told Anne. 'If you can just breathe this baby out I don't think you'll tear.'

'I want to get up,' Anne gasped.

Fiona nodded at John and Sue, who helped her back into her squatting position.

'Gravity can only help. Don't push—relax everything,' Fiona reminded Anne as another contraction began.

The head was delivered gently and Sue moved to wipe the baby's eyes and clear the air passages with a suction tube. Fiona grinned as she saw both Anne and John transfixed by the sight of their emerging child.

'Would you like to finish the delivery, John?'

Sue supported Anne, and Fiona guided John's

hands, allowing him to catch his child as the next contraction completed the delivery.

'It's a boy,' John told his wife happily, and he gently laid their newborn on her abdomen.

'And no stitches needed,' Fiona added with satisfaction, doubting whether Anne either heard or cared at that point. She turned to the midwife.

'Clamp the cord when it's stopped pulsating. I'll leave you to it for the third stage, then I'll come and check everyone.' Fiona stripped off her gloves and gown. 'After that we should be able to give this family a bit of peace and quiet.'

Absorbed with their baby, the Smylies didn't notice Fiona slipping from the room.

Martin was still next door with Ellen Whitmore. Fiona gave him Jonathan's message and he glanced at his watch and frowned.

'How are you feeling, Ellen?' Fiona smiled at a much less distressed-looking young woman.

Ellen smiled back, a little tightly. 'The epidural is fantastic. I'll still be very glad when it's over, though.'

'Won't be too long now.' Fiona turned as the door opened and Jonathan entered. He nodded at Martin, who moved over to the door.

'They'll be expecting you in Theatre in a few minutes. Everything under control here?'

'Protracted first stage until acceleration. Things moved quickly for a while but we've stalled again at second stage. I think we'll need a rotation and forceps shortly.'

Jon's beeper went as Fiona joined the two men. The midwife was checking Ellen's pulse and blood pressure. Her partner was feeding her some small chips of ice.

Jon tapped his beeper. 'That'll be the probable emergency Caesar arriving.' He looked at Fiona with concern and spoke quietly. 'Are you confident to cope here?'

'Yes. I've done two before, though not on my own.'

Martin nodded. 'She's great—a natural.'

Jon smiled fondly. 'Must have been all that practice with the lambs. Call me if you need to.'

'I'm off to Theatre, then,' Martin said cheerfully. 'Maybe I'll catch you later.'

Jon shook his head as he followed his registrar. 'They weren't kidding when they said it got busy around here, were they?' He smiled quickly at Fiona. 'I'll buy you a cup of coffee later, if we ever get the chance.'

The chance didn't come until mid-afternoon, when Fiona and Jonathan found themselves heading for the kitchen at the same time.

'Another caffeine fix?' he enquired.

'You bet.' Fiona grinned. The thrill of the day's successful cases so far was still with her, and her antagonism towards her new boss was, for the moment, forgotten. 'I'll do the honours this time. If we're lucky we'll get a whole five minutes.'

'You seem to be thriving on it,' Jon commented.

'I love it,' Fiona admitted, reaching for the mugs. 'When something like that forceps delivery goes well, I get a real buzz out of it.'

'I got the rundown from Christine,' Jon said. 'She

was pretty impressed with your competence. Said she'd never seen a junior registrar do so well.'

'She's a great midwife.' Fiona handed Jon a steaming mug. 'In fact, the way this place runs so competently is largely down to the midwives, I think.' She sipped her coffee. 'Shall I tempt fate and make us a sandwich?'

'You can try.' Jon glanced at his watch. 'They'll be calling me up to Theatre for the Caesar shortly. Are you free to assist?'

'Oh, yes, please,' Fiona replied eagerly. 'I think everything's under control here for a bit. I know it's difficult for the patients, but *I love Caesareans*.'

Jonathan laughed. 'Your enthusiasm is admirable.' He watched as Fiona cut slices of cheese and then spoke softly.

'I always knew you'd turn out to be a rather special woman, Fiona Donaldson.'

Fiona paused, dismayed by the wave of sensation that flowed through her body. It was something she hadn't felt in a very long time but she recognised it only too well.

'Not only special, but extraordinarily beautiful as well.' Fiona put down the knife. They were standing close together in the small kitchen, and when she turned they were easily within touching distance.

The eye contact was almost a physical caress in itself, and Fiona couldn't breathe as she watched the confusion in Jon's expression. She had seen it once before and it had been enough to feed her dreams for many years. It was also the basis for her assumption that Jonathan had known exactly now she'd felt about him, and therefore *must* have been aware of how much he had hurt her.

Watching Fiona muster sheep single-handed hadn't quite been the last time Jonathan had seen her. True, it had been the day before he was to leave the farm for the last time and head off overseas, but there had been a far more memorable encounter after that.

They had taken the horses out again late that evening, just the two of them. The reason given had been that they were going to look for stragglers from the muster, but it had been proving a difficult evening for Fiona, with the imminent farewells, and she'd simply wanted to escape.

The family had been concerned about her unusually withdrawn mood, although Laura had thought she knew the reason well enough, and there had been general relief when Jonathan had offered to go with Fiona to try and cheer her up. But the fast pace she'd set had precluded any conversation.

He'd seemed glad when she'd finally dismounted to give her horse a rest and he'd joined her, sitting on the brow of a hill that overlooked the farm and surroundings.

'This must be the most beautiful place on earth.'

Fiona's gaze had swept the rugged peaks of the Remarkables, ominous as the fading daylight turned them into silhouettes, over the rolling acres of high country tussock and down to where the quiet dark expanse of Lake Wakitipu bordered their property. The dense planting of trees obscured the homestead far below them but Fiona had been able to just make out a figure—probably her father—going out to feed the dogs.

'I'm sure it is,' she had finally responded quietly.

They'd been sitting so close together that their thighs were touching, and they were holding hands.

That had been nothing unusual. They had held hands occasionally when alone since Fiona was eleven. What had been unusual was the way Jonathan had looked at her.

'You're growing up, Pen,' he had said, his tone almost bewildered, as if he were wondering where the years had gone.

She had said nothing, simply waiting for the inevitable and magic moment when his lips touched hers. A gentle, brief kiss. But, after moving away, Jonathan had kissed her again, and this time the still-leashed passion had been obvious to them both.

Clearly confused, Jonathan had scrambled to his feet.

'It's getting dark, Pen. We'd better get home.' He'd swung himself up into the saddle. 'I must say I haven't seen any stray sheep.'

'I wasn't looking for them,' Fiona had replied inaudibly.

And now the look was there again. The recognition of her sexuality and, with it, an almost palpable desire. Again, she waited for the inevitable physical contact, painfully aware that the huge gap in time and all the bitter emotions had not lessened the excitement. It had, in fact, heightened it considerably.

The sound of Jonathan's beeper was unbearably strident. The atmosphere was shattered. Fiona struggled between feeling relieved and crushingly disappointed.

'That'll be for us,' Jonathan said thickly. He cleared his throat. 'Let's go.'

Fiona noticed his expression of extreme regret as they left the kitchen but had to laugh as he glanced behind them.

'Shame about those sandwiches.'

CHAPTER THREE

SEVEN-THIRTY a.m.

Fiona glanced at her watch as she replaced the telephone receiver and then smiled wearily at Martin.

'Only another thirty minutes and we'll be off call.'

'Terrific,' Martin enthused. 'Then we'll just have our post-acute ward round, the extras to take to Theatre, the rest of the post-acutes and then—what is it again? Oh, yes, a colposcopy clinic this afternoon.'

Fiona stifled a yawn. 'Well, we wouldn't want life to get boring.' She stood up and stretched, glad of the loose-fitting pale blue theatre trousers and top. She had been wearing them ever since the Caesarean yesterday afternoon, due more to lack of opportunity to change than preference. For warmth she had on a cotton coat in a darker shade of blue that tied at the waist, and her comfortable trainers were covered with the disposable theatre bootees.

'That reminds me,' she added. 'That was Theatre on the phone. They'll be ready for Ginette Shaw in twenty minutes.'

Martin got to his feet wearily. 'Let's make a start on the round down here, then. Looks like Jonathan's having a sleep-in.'

'Don't bet on it.'

The atmosphere in the room suddenly seemed to crackle into life at the familiar voice behind them. Fiona had a flashback to the encounter in the kitchen yesterday. Her tiredness was instantly replaced by a much stronger physical state, which Fiona dismissed as the effects of overwork. She took a deep breath, before turning to greet her boss.

'Good morning, sir,' she said a little too cheerfully, gathering up the stack of case notes on the bench. 'Slept well?'

'Better than you two, by the look of it,' Jonathan answered. 'How come you didn't call me in?'

Martin had been watching Fiona carefully, but if he noticed her reaction to Jonathan's entrance he gave no sign of it.

'It's that special course we did at medical school,' he told Jonathan seriously. 'The consultant's sleep is sacred until all other means have failed.'

Jonathan was smiling. 'No failures, then, I take it?'

'All pretty straightforward. We're just going to check on Ellen Whitmore. She's Fiona's assisted delivery from yesterday morning.'

'And we have Ginette Shaw ready for Theatre in fifteen minutes,' added Fiona. 'She came in at five this morning, transferred from a district hospital. Post-partum haemorrhage, running a temperature. We've started her on IV antibiotics and will be doing a D and C, probably for retained portion of placenta.'

'Good.' Jonathan nodded.

'Apparently the midwife thought there was something a bit odd about the placenta, but didn't bother informing the doctor until the patient began running a temperature and bleeding.'

'Good grief.' Jonathan shook his head at this information from Martin.

Fiona relaxed as any personal thoughts were buried by the professional discussion.

'It was a home delivery,' she put in. 'We gather

there was a bit of distraction, with the other kids trying to be helpful.'

'Sounds like a circus,' commented Jonathan.

'I think Mrs Shaw is quite pleased at the thought of a few days' rest in here,' Fiona smiled.

They went in to see Ellen Whitmore.

While Martin and Jonathan checked the chart and talked to Ellen, Fiona went to the small bundle lying in the plastic crib at the bedside. For a minute she just gazed at the tiny face of the sleeping baby, then she put out a finger and stroked the downy head.

The marks from the forceps were already receding and the baby looked healthy and contented. She smiled, remembering the thrill of the successful outcome to the difficult delivery. Then Fiona became aware she was being watched and realised that her colleagues were satisfied with the condition of their patient. She grinned at Ellen, who returned her smile.

'It's nice to see a doctor who really enjoys babies.'

'She can't wait for one of her own,' Martin said teasingly.

They excused themselves and paused to replace Mrs Whitmore's notes in the office before the registrars headed off to Theatre.

'Some independently-minded women just choose a father for their child without bothering about marriage.'

Fiona recognised the tone in Martin's voice and responded with equal sincerity.

'Is that so?'

'I happen to know of an excellent candidate,' Martin continued. 'Not bad-looking, a modicum of intelligence, no family history of heart disease, high blood pressure or diabetes—'

Fiona could not continue to keep a straight face. 'Don't call me, Martin. I'll call you.'

'I'll keep my answering machine on,' he promised.

Fiona's laughter was stilled instantly when she caught the expression on Jonathan's face. The joke had clearly been lost on him, and suddenly it didn't seem very funny to Fiona either. She felt the edge of a now-familiar tension tighten around her and she cleared her throat.

'Do you need me upstairs, Martin, or should I carry on with the round?'

Martin, too, had sobered. 'You stay,' he decided. 'You can fill Jonathan in on everyone just as well as I can.'

Having checked on their Caesarean case from the previous afternoon, Fiona picked up the notes and informed Jonathan of a woman who had been admitted at 2 a.m. with a threatened premature labour, raised temperature and pain on urination.

Jonathan leafed through the results of blood and urine tests which had just been faxed through to the ward.

'You were right to start the antibiotics. White cell count is well up in both blood and urine.'

'We're running an IV salbutamol infusion,' Fiona said, 'and we were going to discuss with you whether to give steroids for the baby's lung development, but things seem to be settling. Contractions are less frequent and the mother's temperature has dropped.'

'How many weeks is she again?'

'Just over thirty-three. Ultrasound a week ago gave an estimated weight of around four and a half pounds.'

'We'll sit tight for the moment, then,' Jonathan

said. 'Even if we can't prevent labour the baby should be fine. It might well be over five pounds by now. The cut-off point for steroids is generally about thirty-four weeks. Anyway, let's go and have a look at her.'

There was time for a quick cup of coffee after the visit, and Jonathan shook his head as Fiona slumped wearily into a chair.

'Did you say that last case came in at 2 a.m.?'

Fiona nodded.

'Have you had any sleep at all?'

Fiona shook her head.

'Have you been home?'

'No.' Fiona sipped her coffee and smiled. 'You certainly know how to make coffee. I feel better already.'

But Jonathan still looked anxious. 'What about Belle? Don't you need to get home to feed her and things?'

'She's fine,' Fiona assured him. She felt irritated that Jonathan seemed to consider she might not be taking adequate care of her pet. Her tone became defensive. 'When I get stuck I ring Laura. Alan picks Belle up on his way home and they look after her. She loves the kids.'

'Hmm.' Jonathan nodded and then glanced at Fiona. It was a calculating look, and Fiona felt instantly suspicious, but then Jonathan simply grinned at her.

'You certainly seem to have your life well sorted out.'

'I certainly have,' Fiona agreed firmly.

The colposcopy clinic seemed interminable, and by the time Fiona switched off her Dictaphone, having finished the final report, it was late. The outpatient and other medical staff had long since departed. Fiona slowly tidied her desk and gathered her belongings.

'At least I won't be a junior registrar for ever,' she muttered to herself. 'It'll just feel like it.'

Her spirits lifted when she eventually parked outside her sister's home to collect Belle. She knew she would be welcomed and fed. She also knew she could forget her current level of stress, at least temporarily.

Laura's greeting at the door was indeed enthusiastic—unusually so—but Fiona's attention was immediately diverted by the four-year-old twins, Jack and Sarah. They each had one of her hands and were pulling in opposite directions, both wanting to show her something of extreme importance.

'You'll never guess—' Laura began. Her voice was lost in the general babble of children's voices. Fiona dropped to a crouch to greet the small boy who was banging a toy truck on her foot.

'Hullo, Michael. Why aren't you in bed?'

'He had to wait up to see his Fee.'

Fiona looked up at her brother-in-law's amused tone, and promptly lost her balance. She sat on the floor, only to be engulfed by the delighted children.

'Come on, Fee,' demanded Jack. 'I want to show you the rocket I made at kindergarten today. It really goes.'

'Wow!' Fiona looked impressed.

'No. I want a story,' protested Sarah.

'I've got some pizza in the oven for you,' Laura said firmly. 'Come on, kids. Stop squashing your aunt.'

'Hey, Fee.' Jack bounced on Fiona excitedly. 'We've got a ghost in the kitchen.'

'Yeah?' Fiona made an appropriately scared face.

'That's what Mummy said he was. Come and see.'

'OK.' Fiona made an attempt to rise but failed as Belle suddenly appeared to welcome her mistress. She laughed helplessly and held up a hand, hoping Alan would assist her. The grip was firm and she was pulled easily to her feet but not by Alan.

'Hullo again.'

Fiona's mouth dropped open. 'What the hell are you doing here?'

'That's our ghost!' shrieked the twins, in unison for once.

Jonathan laughed. Laura and Alan both said something at the same time and Fiona felt overwhelmed by the gaiety. Then she felt a surge of anger.

'I know we have to work with each other,' she snapped. 'But does that also mean I have to see you every time I'm off duty as well?'

There was a sudden silence. Everyone stared at Fiona in astonishment. Fiona was glaring at Jonathan, who was looking uncomfortable.

Laura nudged Alan, who quickly scooped up Michael. 'Bedtime, kids.'

'Oh, but—'

'No buts.' Alan herded the twins firmly with his free arm. 'Fee will come and say goodnight when you're in bed.'

'Yes, I will.' Fiona smiled at the bewildered children. 'I promise.' She kicked herself inwardly for destroying the happy atmosphere, but her smile vanished as she glanced back at Jonathan.

'I'm not really chasing you around.' Jonathan flashed his one-sided grin placatingly. 'I didn't know you'd be coming.'

'You did,' Fiona said accusingly. 'I told you Belle

was here.' She remembered the calculating look he had given her at the time, and tightened her lips. 'I suppose you used your considerable charm again on that person in management to get the address?'

'That's right.' Jonathan's smile was confident again and his arrogance incensed Fiona.

'We couldn't believe it when he turned up on the doorstep,' Laura added quickly. She put her arm around Fiona and moved her towards the kitchen. 'Come on, we managed to keep the kids' fingers off your pizza.'

'Not without a struggle.' Jonathan laughed behind them, and Laura joined in the laughter.

Fiona sensed that Jonathan's welcome and acceptance here had been instant. The thought was confirmed as Laura smiled at Jonathan as she put a plate of pizza in front of Fiona.

'Don't let me forget to give you Daniel's number. He's going to be so thrilled to hear from you.'

Fiona nibbled at her food. She wasn't feeling hungry. Laura excused herself at the sound of a baby's wail and Fiona found herself alone with Jonathan. He sat down on the other side of the table.

'What's the problem, Pen?' he asked quietly. 'I thought we were friends again. I thought I'd explained everything. I know I apologised.'

'You apologised,' Fiona conceded, 'but you explained nothing. And you assumed we were friends again.'

'You said you weren't interested in any excuses.' Jonathan's grin surfaced briefly. 'You're a hard woman, Fiona Donaldson.'

Fiona sniffed. She fed the rest of her pizza to Belle, who was lying beside her chair. Looking up, she found Jonathan staring at her with a very serious expression.

'My marriage ran into trouble fairly quickly, Pen. I felt like a failure and didn't want to admit it to the people I cared most about. I was hoping things would come right. The longer I left it the harder it was to undo. I suppose I threw myself into my career and let it take over my life.'

He reached across the table to grasp Fiona's hand and waved his free hand towards the muffled sounds of the children's voices upstairs. 'You're the only family I'll ever have. Right now, I can't believe I was stupid enough to do without the support you could have given me.' His grin reappeared. 'How's that for an excuse? Will it do?'

Laura came into the kitchen, carrying Jennifer, the baby. 'The twins are refusing to sleep until you've said goodnight,' she told Fiona.

Aware of her sister's curious gaze, Fiona withdrew her hand from Jonathan's. She couldn't doubt his sincerity, despite the final flippant comment, and she smiled as she rose. 'I guess it'll do,' she told Jonathan. 'For the moment.'

By the time Fiona returned downstairs Jonathan had left.

'Alan's given him a ride back to the hospital,' Laura informed her.

'Oh.' Fiona felt miffed at his leaving without saying goodbye and her sister laughed at her expression.

'What's going on, Fee? You bite his head off when you see him and now you're cross because he's gone. Anyone would think you're in love with the man.'

'That's ridiculous!' Fiona was outraged by the suggestion. She glared at her sister. 'I've got to go.'

Laura spoke quietly 'It wasn't so ridiculous the last time he was around, was it? Or did you think I hadn't noticed?'

Fiona clicked her fingers and Belle moved quickly to her side. 'That was a long time ago, Laura. Ancient history—forget it.'

Laura followed her to the door. 'I had, actually—until tonight,' she persisted gently. 'The question is, have you?'

Fiona eyed her sister. 'Perhaps I hadn't forgotten,' she conceded. 'But it's been well buried. And as far as I'm concerned that's where it's going to stay.' She smiled wistfully as she turned away. 'It's really the best place for dead things.'

CHAPTER FOUR

THE hospital cafeteria was a vast bustle of activity.

It always made Fiona think of a central railway station in rush hour. People hurried out, singly or in groups, looking as if they should have been somewhere else five minutes ago, passing similar groups who were eagerly coming in, looking hopeful at the prospect of a break and something to eat. The row of telephones against one wall often had queues beside them, beepers went off almost continuously and there was a hubbub of conversation and laughter.

Everybody ate there—from the orderlies to the consultants, hospital management staff and patients' relatives who were given passes when needed. The food was plentiful and varied. At peak times the huge room was vibrant and alive. Fiona thoroughly enjoyed going to the 'caf', though she didn't seem to manage it very often.

Today she had come alone. She collected a wooden tray and stood in the queue to file past the cabinets of food selections. In between making her choices, Fiona scanned the room hopefully. Despite herself, she was disappointed, though hardly surprised, not to see Jonathan anywhere. Laura's comment had made for another night of broken sleep, and Fiona had finally had to admit to the depth of the unresolved conflict she had.

She couldn't decide exactly what her feelings for Jonathan Fletcher were, but their intensity meant she was going to have to deal with them. Whatever opportunity presented itself she intended to use. Perhaps when she understood her feelings she would then be able to put them to rest.

Arriving at the check-out, Fiona paid for her unbuttered blueberry muffin, fresh fruit and orange juice, pausing for a long moment for one last scan. Seeing Martin Cox sitting with two of the paediatric registrars, Fiona made her way to the corner table they occupied. She was due to begin a run on Paediatrics next, and was always keen for conversation about the speciality, but as she set down her tray they both rose and excused themselves.

Fiona smiled. 'It can't be something I said, at any rate.'

Jill Banks, a senior paediatric registrar, returned her smile.

'Sorry, Fiona. We're just late, as usual. There'll be plenty of time to catch up tonight, I hope. See you then.'

'Tonight?' Fiona queried, but Jill was already joining the outward flow.

'Looks like you're stuck with my company,' Martin said gloomily. 'Bad luck.'

Fiona sighed theatrically. 'Don't know if I can stand it.' She unloaded her tray, waiting for the next stage of verbal sparring, but Martin was silent and Fiona looked at him specutively.

'What's up?'

'Nobody loves me.'

Fiona snorted into her orange juice, almost spilling it. She set it down carefully and arranged her face into sympathetic lines. 'Must be tough.'

'You wouldn't know.' Martin took a large mouthful of the chow mein he had before him.

'I see you haven't gone off your food.'

'Would you throw yourself at me if I went on a public fast?'

'No.'

'May as well eat, then.' Martin still seemed to be lacking his usual level of humour, and Fiona decided to change the subject.

'What did Jill mean about tonight?'

'It's the welcome party for your boyfriend.' Martin glared at Fiona suspiciously. 'I was sure you'd have the first invitation. One of the paediatric consultants, Doreen Roberts, is having it at her place. 8 p.m. tonight.'

'I haven't heard a thing. Maybe I'm not invited.'

It was Martin's turn to snort and Fiona sighed again. This time it was genuine. Jonathan had made assumptions about her relationship with Martin, and now Martin was making similar assumptions about Jonathan. Considering there was nothing actually going on in either case, it was far too complicated for a lunch-break.

'Have you heard about the job in Edinburgh yet?' Fiona tried a new conversational tack. Martin was desperate to land a consultant position in his chosen speciality, but the competition was keen. The application to Edinburgh was the latest in a series he had made in his fourth year as a senior registrar.

'No. But I'm sure they'll turn me down too.'

Fiona was tempted to kick Martin's shin under the table, and nearly did so. Instead she spoke brightly. 'Ginette Shaw is doing brilliantly. I think we could discharge her tomorrow. Her tempt's normal, no further bleeding and she's feeling great.'

Martin nodded.

'I've discharged Ellen Whitmore and told Mrs Cook she can probably go home soon. That's the prem labour that seems to have settled completely.' Between bites of muffin, Fiona ran through the list of inpatients she had spent the morning checking on. Then she smiled. 'That's it for me. How was Gynae Outpatients?'

'Awful,' Martin responded. 'One obvious cervical carcinoma. A fifty-three-year-old woman who's had irregular bleeding for years but has never mentioned it to a doctor. Assumed it was a normal menopause. She hadn't had a smear for about six years either. It's at least stage three, possibly four. I've admitted her for an ultrasound, IVP and possible pelvic CT scan, but my instinct tells me it may just be a case of handing her on to the oncology team'.

Fiona's sympathy was unmistakably genuine this time. 'Oh, Martin, that's awful. No wonder you're feeling down.'

'That was just the first case,' Martin said grimly. 'The worst was a twenty-one-year-old. She was thrilled to be pregnant for the first time, her GP made a routine abdominal examination and sent her straight in to us. She's probably got an advanced ovarian tumour.'

'She's unusually young,' Fiona commented. 'The prognosis isn't great if that's what it is, is it?'

'No.'

'And the pregnancy will complicate any treatment.'

'I'll discuss it with the boss,' Martin said heavily.

'It's a tough one.' He pushed his plate away and, surprisingly, smiled at Fiona.

'Sorry. I'm not great company, am I?'

'You don't have to be,' Fiona told him. 'The pressures in this job are huge, both emotional and physical. We can't expect to always stay on top of it. We do get some amazingly positive cases too, you know.'

'I know.' Martin drained his coffee-cup. 'I'm probably just tired.'

'You and me both,' agreed Fiona. 'That was a rough night on call this week. Even if I do get an invitation, I don't have any intention of going out tonight.'

'Me neither,' said Martin firmly.

They had to laugh when they both arrived at the same time. Fiona eyed the large house belonging to paediatrician Doreen Roberts and grinned at Martin.

'I couldn't really turn down the invitation of someone who's going to be my boss in a few months' time, could I?'

'Of course not,' Martin concurred. 'And I thought I'd better chaperon you with your present boss.'

'Oh, give it a rest, Martin.' Fiona's tone was exasperated. 'There's nothing going on.' She started to walk down the path.

'But you'd like there to be, wouldn't you?'

Fiona turned, startled. 'No,' she said emphatically. 'Absolutely not.'

Martin smiled at her expression. 'Perhaps I know you better than you know yourself,' he said calmly. He tapped his forehead. 'I'm tuned in.' He caught up with Fiona and put his arm around her shoulders. 'If that's what you want, then all the best. I hope it works out.'

Fiona was silent. First Laura and now Martin. Was there something so obvious to them that she couldn't see herself?

'Well, there's always me to fall back on,' Martin continued cheerfully. He sounded more like himself than he had all day. 'I haven't given up. Did I tell you how fantastic you look?'

'No. You were a bit slow today,' Fiona grinned and relaxed a little. 'But thank you. You do wonders for my ego.'

Fiona had made an effort for this evening, despite her weariness. Her top was pale gold, a flowing smock which would have made her pale skin look insipid except that it was partly unbuttoned to reveal a body suit that matched her leggings in a much darker shade of gold.

Her magnificent length of hair was loose apart from two thin braids she had made at each side, drawing them back with a clip to hold the rest of her mane in place like a headband. Her make-up was minimal, as usual, but effective, and her lack of sleep had shadowed her eyes, making them seem even larger than normal. There was an air of vulnerability about her that Martin had never before been aware of. As far as he was concerned, she could not have been more attractive. He sighed heavily.

Fiona pushed the doorbell. 'Chin up. You look great too.'

'I know,' Martin said sadly. 'Bit of a waste, isn't it?'

The informal party was well attended and had been in full swing for some time when the two registrars arrived. Fiona accepted a glass of wine and began a slow move in the direction of the supper tables. She had missed dinner and was extremely hungry. Her progress was hampered by frequent greetings and pauses for conversation, and thirty minutes passed before she was even halfway to the food. Fiona was delighted to see Martin approach, carrying a large tray of savouries. She took two, balancing them carefully on a paper napkin.

'Nice to see you earning your keep,' she told him approvingly.

'I know my place,' Martin said solemnly.

'Fiona! I'm glad you made it.' Jill Banks turned and drew Fiona into a small group of people. 'I must introduce you to these folk—you'll be working with them soon enough.'

Fiona was happy to co-operate, and between bites of her large vol-au-vents she met some of the management and nursing staff. She joined in with their lively conversation about the mechanics of running a busy paediatric department.

Fiona had been acutely aware of Jonathan's presence ever since she'd entered the house, and he had acknowledged hers by way of a nod or wave several times. It seemed that every time her gaze wandered their eyes met, and Fiona was disconcerted by the way it kept happening. It was entirely accidental, as far as she was concerned, but she knew the inference most men would take from the repeated eye contact.

Even if her body *had* betrayed her by the waves of desire she had experienced, it wasn't as if she was the only female in his present orbit to be affected by his physical attractions. And she was certainly not going to be as blatant as some of the nursing staff and give Jonathan Fletcher the satisfaction of knowing about it. Or give herself the opportunity of making a fool of herself again.

Once aware of the situation, it was really quite easy for her to avoid looking at Jonathan and to keep out of his way because he was the centre of attention and there was a competitive edge to inclusion in his immediate group. Despite having no wish to compete, Fiona eventually found she had gravitated to the outskirts of the group surrounding the guest of honour.

Fiona helped herself to a couple of club sandwiches the next time Martin came past, and then watched him as he continued to hand around the sandwiches, noticing how the eyes of women were drawn to him. It was only a matter of time before he found what he was looking for.

Martin had stopped to offer the last sandwich on his tray to Lisa Huntly, an ultrasound technician whom Fiona knew well from her recent training sessions. She was petite, dark and rather vivacious, and Fiona wondered if Martin was aware of how openly admiring the gaze was from his companion.

Taking a bite from her own sandwich, Fiona turned her attention to the conversation around her. She planned to wait for a break and then excuse herself. She really was very tired.

The group at present consisted mostly of consultants, and one was congratulating Jonathan on the number of research papers he'd had published. Fiona recognised Peter Mackwell, a senior paediatrician and dignified older consultant.

'I must say, your CV is quite remarkable for a young chap like yourself, Jon,' Peter continued. 'An MD and a Ph.D. Very impressive.'

Fiona was unaware that Jonathan had gained these prestigious post-graduate degrees. She was also impressed.

'I found I had a lot of time on my hands,' Jonathan said easily. 'Research was a good way to keep me out of mischief.' His eyes sought Fiona's and she caught the ghost of a wink. Only she would understand the reference to the fact that his life had been purposefully buried in academic as well as clinical commitments.

Doreen Roberts joined the group, carrying a bottle of wine, and proceeded to top up glasses.

'I saw you present a paper at the conference in Milan two or three years ago,' she told Jon as she filled his glass. 'You were introducing the subject of laparoscopic hysterectomy.' She shook her head. 'I've never heard such a big laugh as you got—and I've never forgotten the story.'

Jonathan gave his one-sided grin. 'I hasten to point out it was only the introduction to my presentation that was amusing—not the entire paper.'

This brought a laugh in itself, but Doreen's comment had aroused everybody's curiosity and she was asked to repeat the anecdote. Doreen waved the now-empty wine bottle in Jonathan's direction.

'I'm sure Jon can tell it much better than me.'

'I doubt it will live up to this build-up,' Jon commented. 'I just referred back to the first abdominal hysterectomy, which was performed by a Charles Clay in 1843. The patient survived the surgery, which was done in Clay's own home, and was doing well. The nurses unfortunately dropped her when they were changing the sheets two weeks later and she promptly died.' He waited until the laughter faded. 'Probably due to infection or a pulmonary embolism but—what the hell—it makes a good story.'

Doreen was moving away. 'Please help yourselves to something to eat. I'm just going to open another bottle.' She smiled at Jonathan and it was then that Fiona remembered Doreen was single. An accomplished paediatrician and an attractive woman, Doreen was clearly finding Jonathan an interesting guest.

'I'm really looking forward to these training sessions, Jon. You're starting next week, I hear?'

'That's right. We've lined up a laparoscopic treatment of endometriosis with an argon beam coagulator, and a couple of laparoscopically assisted vaginal hysterectomies.'

'LAVH is the catchphrase of the moment,' said Peter Mackwell. 'I'll be interested to see if it lives up to its reputation.'

'You've got a good set-up here, I gather,' Jon said enthusiastically. 'Video relay to an observation room. We should be able to accommodate everyone who's interested and still leave some room in the theatre for the patient.'

This drew another laugh.

'Save me a front row seat.' Doreen's smile was again directed at Jonathan, and Fiona wondered why she had never noticed before just how attractive Dr Roberts was. She was not as tall as Fiona, but was equally slim. Her blonde hair was short and the neat style added to her confident manner. She was a woman in her thirties, well established in her career, and she gave the impression that she knew exactly where she was going in life. Did Dr Roberts's plans now include Jonathan Fletcher?

Suddenly Fiona felt unbearably weary, and didn't manage to stifle her yawn with any great success.

'Keeping you up, are we?'

It was the first direct word she'd had from Jonathan all evening, and Fiona glanced at her watch before smiling ruefully. It was nearly 11 p.m.

'I *am* tired,' she confessed.

'I'm not surprised,' Jonathan responded. 'With the kind of workload you cope with. I feel like I could sleep for a week myself. Must be jet-lag—and advancing age. At least you've got youth on your side.'

'I am twenty-four now,' Fiona replied. She stifled a smile. 'But I won't argue. Thirty-two *is* getting a bit over the hill.'

'Thanks.' Jonathan laughed ruefully. 'I suppose I asked for that. I'll just have to hope I can cope. What's on for you tomorrow?'

Fiona brightened. 'I'm going to do the amniocentesis tests for the antenatal clinic with Martin. The afternoon is just a catch-up on all our inpatients, so hopefully should be quiet. Then it's the weekend. We'll have to make the most of it—we're on call the weekend after that.'

She excused herself as a new knot of people began to form around Jonathan. She looked for Martin to say goodnight but paused when she spotted him. Still holding the sandwich tray, which had long since been emptied, he was sitting beside Lisa, engaged in earnest conversation. Deciding against disturbing the pair, Fiona smiled and let herself out of the house.

Judging by his fresh appearance the next morning, Jonathan had coped well with his late night, despite his age. Fiona inclined her head to invite him into the room where she was working.

'I could use your expertise,' she said, 'then I won't have to wait to interrupt Martin.'

'My pleasure.' Jonathan came over and looked at the ultrasound screen.

'This is Mrs Carter,' Fiona explained. 'We're just about to do an amniocentesis but I'm a little concerned about the position. As you can see, we have quite a low-lying placenta here and the baby's back here.' Fiona moved the cursors on the screen, more for the benefit of Mrs Carter than Jonathan. 'The main pool of amniotic fluid is between them, which makes it a little awkward.'

'There's quite a lot of activity,' commented Jon as he took the transducer and continued scanning. 'The baby may well move to a better position. Or you could come in at an angle down here.' He pressed a point on one side of the patient's abdomen, but continued scanning as he spoke. 'Look, the baby's turned,' he said. 'The back's towards the placenta. You've got a nice space over the limbs now.'

Jonathan moved back and Fiona made a mark on the skin with a pen. She swabbed the area with an antiseptic solution.

'I'm going to inject a small amount of local now, Mrs Carter,' she explained. 'Just the same as you get at the dentist. It will sting for a moment.'

Fiona then reached for the longer needle in the kidney dish. 'Now I'm going to pop the needle into the uterus. You won't feel it on the skin but it might be a bit uncomfortable going through the wall of the uterus. I'll make it as quick as I can.'

Confidently, Fiona depressed the needle, glancing up as Mrs Carter grimaced.

'That's the worst bit over,' she reassured her patient. 'Now we'll check the position of the needle with the ultrasound.' Fiona briefly scanned Mrs Carter's abdomen again.

'Perfect,' said Jonathan.

Fiona smiled. She attached the syringe to the needle and began to carefully withdraw amniotic fluid. The pale yellow liquid bubbled into the syringe.

'How much do you take?' Mrs Carter sounded nervous.

'Only twenty millilitres,' Fiona responded. 'It looks a lot more in a syringe. It's probably only ten per cent of what's in there, and it will replace itself within forty-eight hours.'

The procedure was over in a few minutes and Fiona made one last scan, after sealing and covering the puncture site. She pointed out the baby's beating heart to her patient.

'It all looks fine,' Fiona told her. 'Now it's just a matter of waiting for the results. That usually takes about three weeks.'

Jonathan waited until Mrs Carter had left before he excused himself. 'I've got a meeting with Philip Reece,' he explained. 'I'll catch up with you again later. That was nicely done, by the way. I'm impressed.'

'So am I,' Fiona responded. 'I had no idea of your international reputation and all the post-grad work you've done. It's really quite amazing.'

Jonathan shrugged. 'I told you I threw myself into my career to get over Clare. It's surprising just what you can achieve, doing nothing but work eighteen hours a day seven days a week. Besides, I had the facilities available, the encouragement of some brilliant colleagues and access to some of the best international centres.'

He smiled at Fiona. 'I wouldn't recommend the lifestyle, however. I've run out of steam a bit lately. That's why I thought the break here would be good. I'm really looking forward to this weekend. I plan to do something so completely different I won't even recognise myself.'

'Such as?'

'I haven't decided yet.' Jonathan's one-sided grin was decidedly charming. 'Got any ideas?'

Fiona hesitated thoughtfully. If ever an opportunity was presenting itself, this was it. Her calm voice belied the sudden thumping of her pulse. 'I just might, actually. Wear something comfortable and I'll pick you up at seven tomorrow morning. I'm doing something I think you might enjoy.'

'Seven a.m.! What kind of time is that to start a weekend?'

Fiona had no sympathy. 'You can sleep in on Sunday.' She laughed. 'You might need a rest after tomorrow.'

At precisely 7 a.m. the next morning Fiona pulled her car in to park outside the hospital hostel where Jonathan had his single quarters. She knew he would be ready and waiting. His reliability had always been easy to take for granted, and Fiona had not even thought to question it now. Pleased to see him wearing the old blue jeans and fisherman's rib jersey again, she waved cheerfully and ordered Belle into the back seat of the car.

With her passenger installed, Fiona took the one-way system towards the port hills, quickly leaving the central city behind because of the almost non-existent traffic at that early hour. She noticed Jonathan gazing at the fawn jodhpurs and well-worn riding boots she was wearing.

'This mystery outing, Pen. It doesn't involve some large four-legged animals, does it?'

'How did you guess?' Fiona changed gear as they began the ascent up the hills.

'I haven't been near a horse for more than six years,' complained Jonathan.

'Well, it's just what the doctor ordered, then, isn't it? Something completely different.' Fiona smiled mischievously. She was rather enjoying the lack of confidence he displayed. For the first time since Jonathan had arrived she felt in control of the situation. 'It's just like riding a bike,' Fiona reassured him. 'You don't forget.'

'Bikes are more likely to do what you tell them,' Jon muttered. 'And they don't bite.'

Fiona smiled again but said nothing. She handled her small car easily, speeding through the turns and twists of the road like a rally driver.

'I might fall off.'

'Won't be the first time.' Fiona laughed and then relented. 'Don't fret. I'll give you something totally bombproof.'

They cleared the brow of the hill and were both silent for a few moments, taking in the beauty of the view. The mirror-like waters of the harbour, with its islands and ragged coastline, were spectacular in the early-morning light.

'We're going to a park on the other side of the

harbour,' Fiona told Jon. 'A friend of mine runs a horse-trekking business there, and she lets me come out of hours and have a ride whenever I like. Apart from her own mare, which I ride, the horses are totally trustworthy. You'd have trouble getting a good canter out of most of them.'

Jonathan sounded happier. 'I suppose the business wouldn't last long if the customers were thrown off too often.'

Leaving the hills behind them, they negotiated the many bays around the harbour edge.

'I don't know why you're worried, Jon,' Fiona said. 'You certainly looked out of place the first time we put you on a horse, but you were extremely competent by the time you left.' Fiona giggled suddenly. 'Apart from mustering bareback, that is.'

Jonathan made an offended noise. 'You try staying on a horse without a saddle when it's just put its foot in a rabbit hole.'

'I never saw the rabbit hole.'

'You had your eyes shut,' Jonathan said firmly. He eyed Fiona quizzically. 'You seem different today... happier.'

Fiona was watching for their turn-off. 'I guess I am. Maybe it's getting away from the hospital—or the city. Probably both.'

And maybe, she admitted privately, it was because the anger she had harboured against this man for so long was slipping, being pushed away by feelings that were more mature. Perhaps she was now capable of looking at the situation from a less selfish point of view, possibly even understanding it. Perhaps it was possible to establish a friendship again and bury the past.

Jonathan seemed satisfied by her comment and nodded.

'You don't really fit in—to a big city, I mean.' He watched as Fiona turned off the road onto a long driveway lined with massive oak trees.

'So, what does the future hold for Fiona Donaldson?'

Fiona changed gear, driving slowly under the canopy of trees. 'That's a big question. A family, I hope.'

'Lots of kids?'

'At least six,' Fiona agreed with a grin. Catching the frown on Jonathan's face, she chuckled. 'I guess I'd settle for two.'

'And what about your career?'

'I've really been wondering about that,' Fiona confessed. 'I really miss being near home. Dad tells me there's a job coming up in the Queenstown district hospital. I wish I had ten years' experience under my belt. I suppose I'll head for general practice. At least that's compatible with both raising a family and getting out of the city.'

'What sort of a job is it in Queenstown?' Jonathan queried.

'Bit of everything.' Fiona smiled. 'There's only one resident doctor who works in with the GPs. General surgery, obstetrics and physician all rolled into one. I think it would be perfect. Variety, almost total responsibility and a wonderful place to live.'

'I did general surgery for two years, before heading into Obstetrics,' Jonathan commented.

Fiona pulled to a halt outside a small shed. 'Would you like an application form?' she queried lightly.

Jonathan laughed. 'No. I've established my career and lifestyle. I'm not going to change it.' He sobered suddenly. 'It's too painful wiping the slate clean and making new beginnings. I should know—I've done it often enough.'

Fiona eyed her passenger reflectively. Was he referring to the series of foster homes he had experienced throughout his childhood? Or was it something more recent? She bit her lip.

'Why did your marriage fail, Jon?'

Jonathan avoided her gaze. 'Let's just say I'm not ideal marriage material, shall we? I don't think you'd be interested in all the gruesome details.'

Fiona was very much interested, but Jonathan's tone made it clear that he didn't want to talk about it. She was determined to break this barrier he had drawn over his years away but knew that now was not the time.

'Come on,' she ordered. 'Let's get some fresh air and blow the cobwebs away.'

Unlocking a shed, Fiona selected articles of tack and a bucket of horse nuts. When they went to the paddock they were immediately surrounded by a mob of friendly horses, all eager for the food. Fiona caught and bridled a lively-looking grey mare, and scrutinised the rest.

'Take Harry. He's the big black gelding,' she decided. 'You'll love him.'

Belle watched excitedly as Fiona and Jonathan gave their mounts a quick brush and saddled them.

'Don't forget to check the girth again,' Fiona reminded Jon.

'I haven't forgotten everything.'

Smiling, Fiona went over as he was about to mount. Silently she held the girth strap and gave Harry a none too gentle nudge in the ribs with her knee. The horse let out its breath with a grunt and Fiona tightened the girth by several notches.

'Just his little joke,' she commented cheerfully. 'He likes to let it out when you get on so you slide underneath.'

Jonathan's grin couldn't completely hide his nervousness. 'I know some people like that,' he joked, fumbling with the strap of his hard hat.

'Here, let me.' Fiona reached up and threaded the strap, then pulled it tight. Her hand brushed Jonathan's neck and she was aware of his tension. The look they exchanged made Fiona acknowledge the situation she had set up. She had issued a challenge and Jonathan was determined to meet it.

'Come on.' Fiona swung herself lightly into the mare's saddle. Her mount pranced sideways and Fiona circled to steady her as Jonathan climbed awkwardly onto Harry's back. They began at a walk, with Belle trotting at Harry's heels. As they cleared the wooded area Fiona let her mare trot along the bank of the river, watching over her shoulder to see how Jonathan was coping.

Maybe she had unconsciously hoped that Jonathan would fall off, or somehow make a fool of himself and provide revenge for her own suffering. But now that was the last thing she wanted to happen. His skill in horsemanship was a link to the past—something symbolic that, if broken, would somehow spell the end. The end to what? Fiona wondered, but then shook her head. She didn't understand what she was thinking.

Sighing, she loosened her pressure on the reins and the mare broke into a swift canter. Turning, Fiona saw that Harry had no intention of being left behind.

Seeing the broad grin on Jonathan's face, Fiona laughed delightedly. Now she could really enjoy herself.

For over an hour they rode through the wooded areas, hill tracks and open riverside stretches, cantering or galloping when they had the space, slowing to a trot or a companionable walk when the going was rougher. The conversation was frequent but light, and they both seemed to laugh as much as they talked.

Finally they both dismounted and led the horses quietly through the trees back towards the stable area. Belle jumped into the trough to cool off. Fiona left the horses tied and went to fetch the grooming gear. She heard a shout and turned to see Belle, shaking the water off herself all over Jonathan. He leapt out of her way and almost collided with the laughing Fiona. Jonathan laughed as well, then put an arm around Fiona.

'Thanks, Pen. I haven't enjoyed myself so much in years.'

'You're very welcome.' Fiona twisted in his embrace and suddenly they were face to face and very close. Without hesitation, Jonathan bent his head and kissed her lips gently.

It was the kiss she had relived so many times. He kissed her again with tender softness, and then, with a stifled groan, Jonathan drew Fiona to him as the third kiss unleashed their passion. But it was so much more than the memory as well. Fiona's lips and tongue met his eagerly as she wound her arms around Jonathan's neck and pressed her breasts against his chest. Jonathan's hands travelled down her back to her hips and drew her to him. Close enough that she knew the desire was just as strong for him.

Suddenly the contact was broken. Fiona couldn't be sure who had stepped back. Perhaps they both had. Her lips felt swollen and her body ached with her need. She could see the effort Jonathan was making to control himself. Their eye contact was intense but they remained silent.

Finally Fiona took a deep breath. Silently she handed Jonathan one of the dandy brushes and moved to start work on the mare. If he didn't want to say anything that was fine by her. She needed some time.

It was ironic, really. She had decided to take any opportunity to sort out how she felt about Jonathan Fletcher. Then she'd intended to find some emotional peace. The opportunity had been perfect and, yes, she now understood exactly how she felt. But peace seemed further away than it had ever been.

CHAPTER FIVE

THE routine was now so familiar it was automatic.

Fiona soaped and scrubbed her hands, her thoughts elsewhere. Had it only been a week ago she had been so preoccupied and nervous about her reunion with Jonathan? She smiled grimly to herself, remembering how she had planned to deal with the encounter.

She had planned to be so controlled and professional, to let him know in a mature manner that he was no longer welcome in her life. Perversely, she had been pleased by his persistence in rekindling their friendship, and she had let her control slip. The slip had become a dangerous slide during that ride on Saturday morning, and she had landed with a crash on finding it had happened again.

Or perhaps it had still been there all along, buried under a pile of emotional rubbish. Whatever the case, she was in love with Jonathan Fletcher.

Fiona rinsed her hands, now feeling raw from the unnecessarily lengthy scrubbing. Well, it didn't have to be the end. Surely control could be re-established. She had the choice of whether to let it go any further or not. It was a choice that was making her feel very nervous. And just how much of it was actually hers?

She glanced across at Martin, expecting to be teased for her silence, but he was also quiet. Fiona sighed. She could have done without the heavy atmosphere in Theatre this morning. They had a routine colposuspension and then a cervical suture, but the last case for the morning was the young mother with probable ovarian cancer. Nobody was looking forward to the case and the usual cheerful banter among the staff was absent. Even the tape deck, usually on softly in the background, was silent.

Fiona smiled at Martin as she dried her hands. 'How was your weekend?'

'Good.' Martin returned her smile automatically but then his smile widened. 'It was great.' He seemed about to enlarge on his reply but then stopped abruptly. 'How was yours?'

'Saturday was great,' Fiona said, trying to sound happy. 'I had a wonderful ride in the morning, then spent the evening around at my sister's.' Fiona snapped on her gloves. 'Yesterday I mucked around at home, trying to decide whether to redecorate my house or just sell up.'

'Do you own that house?' Martin seemed surprised. 'I thought you were just renting it. What's the secret to such early financial success?'

Fiona followed Martin into Theatre. She was assisting for this first case and was glad of the opportunity to distract Martin a little from the later case for the morning.

'No great success.' She smiled. 'I'm in a central city area that hasn't achieved any noticeable popularity yet. It's a tiny cottage in dire need of a lot being done to it. And I've got a rather large mortgage.' She watched as Martin made his incision and began a competent dissection towards the bladder. 'I gave up the idea of renting when I found how difficult it was going to be with a dog in tow.'

'Mmm.' Martin's interest in Fiona's property had dissipated. 'We'll probably be doing this laparoscopically soon. I was looking forward to the demonstration.'

Fiona nodded. She moved in and sealed the trickle from a small blood vessel that was obscuring the field. 'Jonathan sounded pretty annoyed about the hold-up in equipment.'

Jonathan had been in Theatre briefly that morning. Most of the conversation had centred on the delay in the planned surgical demonstrations.

Martin chuckled. 'I wouldn't have liked to be responsible for telling him. I don't imagine he takes too kindly to having his plans disrupted.'

'No.' Fiona lapsed into silence again as she watched Martin. She clamped a larger vessel at his direction. Fiona had not seen Jonathan before in the mood he had been in that morning. Purely professional, almost clipped. She wondered whether it had been entirely due to the annoyance of the hold-up in equipment or if it was how he had now decided to approach his relationship with her.

It could simply be the disruption to his programme. Surgeons could often be like that. But Fiona's instinct told her it was more and she didn't like it. If Jonathan was taking control of their interaction then that removed her choice. As difficult as that choice might have been, Fiona still wanted the right to make it.

'Arrogant,' she muttered to herself. 'Typical surgeon.'

'What was that?' Martin shot her a glance.

'Nothing.' Fiona shook her head.

Martin shrugged. 'Right. Let's get these sutures into place.'

Fiona turned her attention back to the task in progress. Jonathan was due back in Theatre at Martin's request to handle the more difficult case of the morning. He had left his registrars earlier with a more cheerful comment.

'I'll leave you both to it,' he had said. 'You make such a fantastic team.'

Fiona had gritted her teeth at that. It had seemed to her a rather blatant dig at their assumed relationship. Martin had simply let it pass.

'He was right, you know.'

'What's that?' Martin glanced up from the careful suturing he was finishing with.

'We do make a good team.'

Fiona knew she was rewarded with a grin, even if she couldn't see it beneath the mask. The operation had gone quickly and smoothly, and the atmosphere in Theatre had lightened a little.

'You can do the next one by yourself,' Martin said. 'I'm going for a coffee.'

'That's what I call teamwork.' Fiona nodded. 'Put your feet up. Enjoy yourself.'

'Actually, I thought I might catch the boss and have a chat about the next case.'

Fiona stripped off her gown and gloves and immediately began to prepare herself for the next case. Inserting the cervical suture was a quick and easy procedure, one that Fiona would normally enjoy. Any lightening of the atmosphere, however, had vanished with Martin's comment and departure. Fiona felt weary suddenly, as though the day should be over, not barely begun.

The change in ambience in the theatre with the presence of Jonathan Fletcher was intriguing. Whether it was due to his professional or personal attitude Fiona couldn't be sure, but an air of optimism pervaded the setting and the staff all responded to it.

With Martin assisting Jonathan, Fiona's role was merely that of an observer, but she was glad to be present. She had never seen Jonathan operating and was highly impressed with both his professional skill and the instant rapport he had with the theatre staff. She and Martin might work well together, but Jonathan had created a team effort that had something extra. It was confident, optimistic—almost determined to succeed. Fiona found herself caught up in it completely.

Anticipating a depressing confirmation of a serious illness in a young mother, the excitement grew with Jonathan's opinion that what they were dealing with was, in fact, Meig's syndrome—an innocent fibroma of the ovary, which gave symptoms mimicking an advanced malignancy. When the frozen section results were phoned through to Theatre to confirm this, the staff let out a cheer that made the anaesthetist grin.

'Careful. Don't wake up my patient.'

The atmosphere really was lifted at that point. Jonathan had all the staff laughing at various surgical anecdotes as he insisted on finishing the surgery himself, right to the final suture. The mood was distinctly jovial as the three doctors stripped off gowns and gloves.

'I'm going to buy you both lunch,' Jonathan told his junior staff. 'And no arguments. We've got plenty of time before Outpatients, and I've been told the Riverside Tavern does a great meal.'

'I never pass up a free meal,' Martin responded. 'Thanks, Jon.'

'Fiona?'

'I should really catch up on dictating some discharge summaries,' Fiona demurred, but she got a nudge from Martin.

'You shouldn't pass up a free meal either. Struggling with that huge mortgage and all the redecorating you're going to do.'

Fiona laughed, embarrassed by the sudden flash of concern she saw on Jonathan's face.

'I'm managing just fine. But, yes, lunch would be nice.'

Jonathan's beeper sounded as Fiona headed for the shower.

'I'll just answer that and I'll meet you over there in ten minutes. Find a table where I can feed the ducks.' His one-sided grin appeared briefly. 'Just in case the food isn't so great.'

The food smelled wonderful, and Fiona glanced at her watch for the tenth time.

'I'm starving. Are we going to keep waiting for him or order our lunch?'

Martin also checked his watch. 'Let's eat. We've only got thirty minutes before the clinic starts.' He waved at a waiter, who hurried over.

'I'll have the fillet steak and mushrooms, thanks.' He raised his eyebrows in Fiona's direction.

'Vegetarian nachos, please.'

'Would you care to see the wine list?'

Martin shook his head. 'I'd love to, but unfortunately we can't. Just mineral water for us both, thanks.'

Their meals arrived within ten minutes. The tavern was almost directly opposite the hospital and was used to serving medical staff in a hurry. Fiona and

Martin had just finished a detailed discussion of their morning's work and observations. Martin was clearly thrilled at the outcome for his young patient and Fiona was delighted to see him look so happy.

They both sobered, however, when Martin asked Fiona if she would come with him later to see Doris Sinclair, his case of advanced cervical cancer. He would have to spend time with Doris and her husband, discussing the test results, a rather poor prognosis and possible treatments, the side-effects of which could well destroy the quality of her remaining life.

Martin wanted to go over it all with Doris himself, before handing her on to the oncology team. Fiona's presence would be both a learning experience for herself and moral support for him. He smiled as he suggested this and then dismissed the dismal subject by raising his glass of mineral water.

'Cheers, Fiona.' Martin gave her a wry smile. 'This is an opportunity I never thought I'd have.'

'What's that?' Fiona scooped up the bean and cheese mixture with a hot corn chip. 'Mmm. This is good. Jonathan doesn't know what he's missing.'

'A meal alone with you, of course. I spent three months trying, if you remember.'

Fiona put down her second chip. Her appetite fled and she smiled without humour. 'Perhaps Mr Fletcher does know what he's missing after all.'

'What do you mean?'

'We've been set up.' Fiona glared crossly around the restaurant. 'I don't think he has any intention of showing up.'

'Oh.' Martin looked embarrassed. 'Sorry, Fiona. Am I getting in the middle of something here? I had the impression it was just the boss rewarding his juniors for a good morning's work.'

'That was what we were supposed to think.' Fiona scowled. 'But we're such a fantastic team, remember?'

'Damn.' Martin was looking even more embarrassed and Fiona redirected her scowl.

'Did you have something to do with this arrangement, Martin?'

'No, of course not. It's just that… Oh, hell.' Martin put down his cutlery and gave Fiona a wry look. 'A week ago I would have given an eye tooth to be part of such a plot, but now—' Martin paused again and took a gulp of water. 'You know I think you're fabulous, Fiona. I've never made any secret of it. But you made it clear a long time ago that wasn't what you wanted.'

Fiona nodded. 'I think you're great, too,' she said with a smile, 'but I haven't changed regarding anything else.'

'Just as well.' Martin picked up his knife and fork and attacked his steak again. 'I told you I had a good weekend. Well, that was an understatement. I spent it with Lisa—you know, the ultrasound technician?'

Fiona nodded again. 'I saw you together at Doreen Robert's place last week.'

Martin grinned. 'That was when it started. I gave her my last club sandwich and—wham!'

'I'm really pleased for you, Martin,' Fiona said warmly. 'I do hope it works out.'

'Oh, it will. I'll make sure of that.' Martin smiled confidently. 'I'm talking serious stuff here. Marriage, kids, you know. The works.'

'Oh, I know.' Fiona pushed a corn chip around her

plate half-heartedly. 'The works' would definitely be her choice, too. But would the package be complete without Jonathan Fletcher?

'We should get going.' Martin frowned at Fiona's plate. 'Aren't you going to eat your lunch?'

She shook her head. 'I'm not really hungry after all.' She stood up. 'So much for the free lunch.'

'Still is for you. I'm paying.' Martin held up his hand to silence Fiona's protest. 'I'm celebrating here.' He gave an anxious glance around him. 'I just hope no one tells Lisa we were off having a romantic lunch together.'

Fiona laughed. 'You can send Jonathan to do the explaining.'

Jonathan nearly collided with the two registrars as they hurried out of the tavern doors. He looked extremely hassled.

'I'm terribly sorry,' he said. 'That call turned out to be from a surgical equipment supplier in the States. I ended up in a teleconference with them, a courier firm and their distribution branch here, trying to sort out the delay. I've only just got off the phone.'

'Not a problem,' Martin reassured him. 'And the food was great.'

Fiona was silent. The story might be plausible but she wasn't going to let him off that easily. She remained silent for the short walk back to the hospital, grateful for Martin's ebullient mood and the animated conversation he kept up with Jonathan about their morning cases. Martin's beeper went as they entered Outpatients and he excused himself to go to a telephone. Jonathan touched Fiona's arm.

'Hey, I rang Daniel last night. Finally got up the

courage to break the silence. Laura gave me his number.'

'That's good. How is he?' Jonathan's touch and friendly tone had stirred Fiona's turbulent emotions into overdrive. She deliberately kept her tone cool.

'He sounded great. Just the same, really, after we got over the initial awkwardness. I ended up running up a thundering phone bill.'

'He must have enjoyed catching up with you.'

'Seems that way,' Jonathan agreed with a grin. 'He's invited me up for a visit the weekend after next.'

'Will you go?' Fiona made an even firmer effort to control the dismay she felt surfacing.

'Of course. I'm looking forward to it. In fact...' Jonathan cleared his throat modestly '...he thinks the Obs and Gynae department up there would be keen for me to talk to them and give a demonstration or two. He's going to see if some arrangements can be made.'

'Must be nice to be famous,' Fiona said coldly. She saw the frown her response generated and she tried to smile placatingly. 'Excuse me. Martin's waving.'

Joining the senior registrar, Fiona could sense Jonathan's gaze following her, but when she glanced back he was already leaving the reception area and moving towards one of the consulting rooms. The antenatal clinic was due to start and, by the look of the waiting room, it was going to be a busy one. Martin, too, seemed eager to get started.

'That was Admitting on the phone, Fiona. A patient of ours has just been sent in by her GP Shirley Cook?'

Fiona nodded. 'The premature labour from last week. We discharged her on Thursday.'

'Well, she's back again. Could you go and see her? Call me or Jon if it looks like she means business this time.'

'OK.' Fiona put on the white coat she had been carrying over her arm, then draped her stethoscope around her neck.

'Catch you later, then.' She grinned at Martin. 'And, seeing as I'm not doing the ultrasound scans this week, you'd better check that there's a competent technician available.'

Martin returned her smile. 'Oh, I intend to. At regular intervals.'

Fiona found her patient in no distress but definitely in labour. Her waters had broken and the contractions, while painless, were strong and occurring at regular fifteen-minute intervals. Fiona took her time over the admitting procedure, knowing that she was covering the same ground as last week but also knowing how important it was to be thorough.

'You've never had a miscarriage or termination of pregnancy before, have you, Shirley?'

'No.'

'And you've never had any kind of pelvic infection or an abnormal smear result in the past?'

'No.'

'No diabetes, episodes of chest pain, kidney problems?'

Fiona obtained a comprehensive medical history, before going over the presenting symptoms.

'Things had settled quite nicely by the time we discharged you. How were you over the weekend?'

'Fine.' Shirley Cook sighed. 'Apart from my husband insisting I stayed in bed so that I had plenty of time to worry about everything.' Her lip trembled. 'Maybe he was right. I got up this morning and it all began again.'

'The contractions?'

'Started with backache, really, though it wasn't bad enough to notice until the contractions began.'

'What time was that?'

'About eight o'clock. Just after Stephen left for work. I still didn't worry—they were so far apart. But then my waters broke...' Shirley began to cry.

'Has someone contacted Stephen for you?' She handed Shirley a tissue.

The midwife had come in to check Shirley's pulse and blood pressure. She nodded at Fiona. 'He's on his way.'

'Good. I'm going to examine you now, Shirley,' Fiona said gently. 'Then I'm going to get our consultant to come and see you. Don't worry. You'll be in the best possible hands.'

It was another thirty minutes before Fiona contacted Jonathan. At least it was easy to keep this contact professional. She gave him a brief reminder of the history and a summary of the present symptoms.

'No results back on the blood we've taken,' she continued. 'But there's no obvious sign of infection. In fact, she still hasn't finished the course of antibiotics we discharged her on. There's no abdominal tenderness but definite uterine irritability.'

'Presentation?'

'No problems there, but I am a bit concerned about the assessment for size. The baby seems small for dates.'

'Amniotic fluid?'

'Not much left, I think. Her waters broke a couple of hours ago and she's been leaking steadily since.'

'Get an ultrasound scan done now,' Jonathan ordered. 'And call me as soon as that's done. I'll contact the neonatal unit. We'll need to liaise with them on this as well.'

Lisa was only too happy to accommodate an emergency scan between clinic patients. As Fiona had feared, the baby's size was smaller than expected, and didn't seem to have changed much from the previous scan of nearly two weeks ago.

'Of course, there's a margin of error with these procedures,' Lisa commented, 'but, even so, I'm surprised there hasn't been more change.'

Jonathan appeared, accompanied by Shirley's husband, as Lisa finished the examination. They quickly discussed the results.

'It looks like your baby prefers to make an earlier appearance than planned, Mrs Cook,' Jonathan said. 'And, judging from these results, it may be better if he does. The growth isn't as much as we'd like to have seen in the last week or so. We could probably delay your labour again but I don't think it would be advisable. We're really in pretty safe territory now at thirty-four weeks.'

He watched as Shirley Cook was helped back into her wheelchair. 'If your baby is in need of special care it shouldn't be for very long.' He looked at Fiona. 'I'm going up to Neonatal now. I'll take Mr and Mrs Cook with me and introduce them to the set-up and staff. Do you want to come?'

Fiona nodded. Jonathan pushed the wheelchair himself and set a good pace as they headed towards the neonatal intensive care unit. Fiona knew it would be a shock for the prospective parents to see some of the tiny scraps of humanity struggling for survival in the unit, but it was also good preparation if their own baby should need assistance.

The staff were welcoming and confident. Somehow Fiona had known it would be Doreen Roberts on duty. The senior paediatrician was delighted to see Jonathan and listened avidly as he introduced the patient.

'At least four pounds.' Doreen smiled at Shirley as he finished. 'You probably won't need us at all. Maybe just a little extra observation for a day or two. Fiona, why don't you give the Cooks a quick tour while I have a chat to Mr Fletcher?'

Fiona complied quietly. They found a baby born at thirty-three weeks who had been just under four pounds, and the mother was delighted to offer some comfort to Shirley.

'You've got nothing to worry about,' she said. 'I was scared stiff when Katy here put in such an early appearance, but she's fine. We've only been here two days and she's already coming out of her incubator for breastfeeding. I'm here with her all day and they wake me in the ward when she's hungry during the night.'

Fiona glanced over her shoulder. Doreen and Jonathan were in animated conversation. Something was giving them plenty to smile about. She was glad to head back to the labour suite.

'There's nothing to indicate we should delay delivery,' Jonathan decided, having examined Shirley himself. 'In fact, I think we should speed things up a little. We'll set up an oxytocin infusion and I'll contact Doreen as soon as we're moving. I'd like to do this delivery myself.' He turned to the midwife. 'We'll need continuous electronic foetal monitoring, and I'd like a scalp electrode available in case we need it.' Jonathan turned his attention to Fiona. 'You're welcome to stay, of course, though I imagine Martin might be glad of some assistance with the clinic.'

'I'll go back to the clinic,' Fiona said crisply. 'I'd rather be of some use.'

Jonathan followed her along the corridor for a few steps and she halted at the touch on her arm.

'I really am sorry about lunch. It was unavoidable.'

'Was it?' Fiona's glance was pointed.

'Of course.' Jonathan frowned. 'You don't think it was deliberate—?'

'I don't know what to think, Jonathan.' Fiona's tone was icy. 'But right now I'd like to get some work done. I'll see you later.'

She didn't see him later, for the antenatal clinic ran well over time because of the disruption. Fiona then spent a harrowing hour with the Sinclairs as they tried to absorb and discuss their devastating news. Fiona was very relieved to finally escape and head for home, picking up a vegetarian burger on the way. The thought of cooking a solitary meal was unusually depressing.

The burger didn't take very kindly to being reheated, but Belle had needed a run in the park and Fiona never went there after dark. They only just made it back to the cottage before it started to rain. Fiona hurried to light the gas fire and feed Belle. In an attempt to stop her thoughts dwelling on Jonathan, Fiona focussed on her surroundings. In her present frame of mind, and with the inclement weather rattling the windows, the poor state of repair was glaringly obvious. Paint was peeling from the ceiling, the windowframes had dry rot, the carpet had large bald patches and the wallpaper was indescribable, both in pattern and condition.

'This place is a dump,' Fiona informed Belle. 'It's no wonder I got it so cheaply. I must have been blind.'

The overall effect, having been concentrated on, was so depressing that Fiona couldn't stand it. She abandoned her half-eaten burger and, going to the nearest wall, pulled on a damaged sliver of paper that dangled free.

To her surprise, the sliver widened dramatically until it covered the whole width of the drop. Holding the end with two hands, Fiona gave a good pull. The length of paper separated itself from the wall right up to the ceiling with a satisfying ripping noise, whereupon it came down—along with a shower of the plaster it had been stuck to—all over Fiona.

She coughed and blinked the plaster dust from her eyes.

'What about that, then, Belle?'

Belle was more interested in finishing the abandoned burger, but Fiona laughed aloud. She couldn't have thought up a better distraction than this. It might even turn out to be the start of a very constructive pastime. At the very least, renovation would add to the value of her property.

Some sheets of wallpaper peeled off easily and others needed some help with the scraping from a kitchen knife, but Fiona attacked the room with enthusiasm. She was halfway along the second wall when Belle's bark alerted her to the knocking at the door.

Jonathan laughed when she opened the door and Fiona did her best to look aloof.

'You've aged considerably since I last saw you,' he explained. 'Your hair's gone white.'

'Oh.' Fiona touched the grit covering her head and grimaced. 'It's plaster dust.' She backed away from the door. 'You'd better come in, I suppose. My hair might set if I get rained on.'

'I don't want to disturb you,' Jonathan said as he entered. 'You're obviously having a good time. I just couldn't leave you thinking what you seemed to be thinking.'

'What was that?' Fiona had kept moving and was already picking at a new area of wall. There was something addictive about this occupation.

'That I deliberately left you and Martin having lunch alone. That I was trying to push you into a romantic situation you didn't want.'

Fiona ripped off a large triangle of wallpaper but remained silent.

'He was right, you know,' Jonathan said conversationally.

'About what?'

'He'd make a good candidate for a father.'

'Give me strength,' Fiona muttered. She spoke slowly and clearly, as though to someone of dubious intelligence. 'Martin Cox is a colleague. He'd like to have been more but that issue was settled some time ago.'

'That's not the impression I've had.'

Fiona bit back a smile. 'Martin just has an irrepressible bounce. He has now, however, fallen in love with someone else. And I'm sure he will, indeed, make a great father.'

'What about the others?'

'Other whats?' Fiona turned an exasperated look on Jonathan.

'Other candidates. There must be a few. Tell me their credentials.'

'Look,' Fiona said sharply, 'it's not really any of your business. I'm quite capable of making my own choices about men, you know. I'm not a child any longer.'

'Oh, I've noticed.'

Fiona caught the undertone and then the hint of a wicked grin. Suddenly flustered, she covered her reaction by attacking a fresh section of wall, scraping furiously at some stubborn remnants of paper.

Jonathan looked around the room. Huge pieces of wallpaper littered the floor, and every surface was covered with a thick layer of dust. 'You're making an amazing mess,' he commented.

'Why don't you offer some help instead of criticism?' Fiona countered. Another satisfyingly large section of paper came away with her tug.

'OK.' Jonathan moved to the last wall and picked the bottom corner of the paper free. 'You do believe me, don't you—about lunch?'

'I suppose so.'

'Have I ever been dishonest with you, Pen?'

Fiona paused and looked at her visitor thoughtfully. 'Not in the past,' she agreed. 'More recently, I couldn't say. You haven't said much.' She pointed to the wall. 'Now get busy. You've got some work to do if you want to earn a cup of coffee.'

Thirty minutes later the room's walls were completely stripped and both Fiona and Jonathan were filthy. They eyed each other and laughed.

'This place looks worse than ever.' Fiona sighed. 'I'll get some rubbish sacks. You can get the vacuum cleaner. There's no point in cleaning ourselves up if we have to come back and sit in here.'

It took another hour to make much impression on the devastation they had created, and Fiona finally shook her head.

'I'm going to have a quick shower. I can't stand all this dust in my hair. You can have one after me, if you like.'

When Fiona returned to the living room, wearing a bathrobe and with a towel around her head, she found Jonathan still busy. Having wiped the dust from all her books and ornaments, he was now brushing Belle. The inviting smell of coffee wafted from the kitchen.

'Shower's all yours,' Fiona offered. 'If I throw your jeans and shirt into the washing machine and dryer they could be ready again in an hour or so.'

'No need to go to all that trouble,' Jonathan protested.

'No trouble,' she responded. 'Besides, I suppose I should make amends for doubting your honesty.'

'Indeed you should,' Jonathan said. 'Right. I'll go and get clean. And while I'm doing that I'll give due consideration to what the rest of your penance should be.'

Fiona suppressed a giggle. Left alone, she knelt by the fire and began to attack her tangled hair with a wide-toothed comb. It was a major task but she felt more than content. She recognised the dangerous state of relaxation that had come after their ride together all those years ago, but felt far too good to want to do anything about it.

When Jonathan entered the room a few minutes later, with only a towel around his waist, Fiona stared, her lips parted. She had not forgotten the impact his partly clad body had had on her during summer swimming sessions in past years, but the reminder was now too powerful in the confines of her small living room.

Added to that, she was seeing him without the ponytail for the first time. The thick, dark waves of his hair almost touched his shoulders. It made him look younger—and different. Yet there was such a strong sense of familiarity about him. He belonged here. Perhaps his presence was the only way her life could feel complete. Not to mention her body.

Jonathan, too, was staring.

'You look like a mermaid, Pen,' he said softly. 'Sitting on a rock and combing your tresses.' He crossed the room in a few short strides and stood beside her.

Fiona found herself trembling. 'Would—would you like some coffee?' she stammered.

'In a minute.'

Jonathan crouched down and picked up a strand of Fiona's hair. He let the soft length of it drift through his fingers.

'God, you're beautiful,' he whispered.

Fiona moved, realising as she did so that the loose bathrobe had exposed her breast. She moved to cover herself but Jonathan caught her hand. Wordlessly she dropped her hand, but instead of pulling her bathrobe across Jonathan eased it back from her shoulder. Bending his head, he first licked then drew the aching peak of her breast into his mouth. Pausing for a long moment, Jonathan stared into Fiona's eyes. Finding whatever answer he was searching for, he carefully undid the tie at her waist and drew her naked body against his.

The tide of passion began slowly and gently. Touch was all they needed to communicate and no words were spoken. Tentatively they both sought to please the other, but the old bonds of trust and friendship were already in place and they soon eagerly rode the waves of desire. At the point of consummation, however, Jonathan suddenly hesitated, as though startled.

Fiona knew why. Reaching to hold him with her legs, she drew him on and into her and again they were both lost. When it seemed that desire and pleasure could get no greater Fiona found her release and knew that both could, indeed, increase. She cried out then, and knew she was answered as Jonathan, too, joined her ecstasy.

For a long, long time they lay together in the warmth of the gas fire, without speaking. It was Jonathan who finally broke the silence.

'That was—I mean, was this the first time for you, Pen?'

Fiona nodded reluctantly, embarrassed.

'Oh, hell.' Jonathan sat up, covering himself with his towel. 'I thought so, but I couldn't believe it. It shouldn't have been me, Pen, for something so special.'

'I couldn't have thought of anyone more perfect.' Fiona also sat up and put on her bathrobe. 'Don't spoil it by apologising, Jon. It was more than I ever believed possible.'

'For me, too,' Jonathan said slowly. 'But it mustn't change anything, Pen.'

Fiona was silent. The whole world had just changed, as far as she was concerned.

'I'm not saying I make a habit of this or anything,' Jonathan said awkwardly. 'In fact, it's probably because I don't that this happened. There hasn't been anyone since Clare. And seeing you sitting there looking so impossibly beautiful…' Jonathan paused and then caught Fiona's hand.

'I've known you, and loved you, since you were a child. It was a very deep but platonic relationship, as far as I knew.' He cleared his throat. 'Though I've wondered just lately whether it was more than that for you.'

Fiona met his gaze timidly. Could she deny something her body had just shouted? Mutely she nodded, and Jonathan squeezed her hand.

'I thought so. I thought that must be why you were so angry with me. I'm so sorry, Pen.'

'Why?' Fiona's word was a whisper.

'Because I can't offer you anything. I know what your future should—and will—hold. And I can't be part of that.'

'Isn't that at least partly my choice?'

'I'm afraid not.' Jonathan let go of her hand and smoothed back his hair.

'And what does my future hold that's so uninviting for you?' Fiona was trying to control the pain his words were inflicting on her but her voice was shaky.

'A home. A family. A lot of children and a lot of love…' Jonathan's voice trailed off. He stared into the fire.

'And you're telling me that isn't something that you want?' Fiona queried softly.

Jonathan looked up and she could clearly see his

pain. 'It's exactly what I want,' he said brokenly. 'What I've always wanted. Perhaps even more than you. I've only had a taste of a real family thanks to you Donaldsons. One foster home after another as a child. It was my dream to belong.

'Wonderful as it was to be included in your family, it still wasn't the end of the dream. I was going to create one of my own. Something invincible. Something that would undo the disaster of my own childhood and give meaning to the rest of my life.'

Fiona rode out the silence. For the first time Jonathan was giving part of himself that had been missing. She didn't dare interrupt the flow that could provide the link.

'It all seemed to be going so well,' Jonathan continued sadly, not looking at Fiona. 'I met Clare. She wanted the same thing. A husband, a home and two point four children.' He laughed bitterly. 'The only problem was I turned out not to supply my side of the equation.'

Now Jonathan's gaze was directly into Fiona's troubled eyes.

'I can't have children, Pen. Bad case of mumps when I was a child. Some time around the third or fourth shift of family. I had blotted it from memory as best I could, along with the rest of my childhood. It all came back with a rush when I saw the results of my sperm test. The odds of me conceiving a child naturally are probably less than one in a million.'

'Things are changing,' Fiona said carefully. 'They're doing some amazing things with reproductive technology now—'

'Don't you think we tried everything?' Jonathan sounded angry. 'Artificial insemination, IVF. Do you know what a physical and emotional grinder it is, going through IVF?' He didn't wait for Fiona to answer. 'It's bloody rough. The stress breaks up a large percentage of couples and Clare resented it all. Resented the pain, the time-consuming appointments, the effects of the drugs. Because it wasn't her fault.

'We discussed adoption, of course, and we eventually decided against it. Clare refused to try any further treatment. We seemed to drift apart, and then...' Jonathan smiled tightly at Fiona '...then she became pregnant. I was over the moon. We had beaten those million to one odds. The dream was still intact.'

Fiona had to break the next silence. It was too tense.

'So what happened?'

Jonathan groaned. 'Clare informed me that the baby wasn't mine.'

'Oh, no!' Fiona's exclamation was one of despair. She could so easily imagine the pain he must have felt.

'She left,' Jonathan went on calmly. 'She married her new bloke—a dentist—the day our divorce was finalised. A week before the baby was born. I moved to Wales and I haven't had any contact with her since. I imagine she's got her two point four children now, and her nice home and husband.'

'So that's why you didn't let Philip talk you into involving yourself with the IVF programme,' Fiona said softly. 'Too many memories?'

'Partly,' Jonathan admitted. 'I got myself heavily involved at the time because I thought it was a solution. To arm myself with knowledge and explore all the possibilities. When it failed it took my enthusiasm with it. Along with a few other things.'

Jonathan leaned towards Fiona and planted a gentle kiss on her forehead.

'I don't want to lose what we've had, Pen. But I've no intention of messing up your life.'

'Children aren't the only reason to be together,' Fiona said quietly. 'Perhaps loving someone and wanting to share your life is more important.'

'It is important but it isn't enough,' Jonathan said slowly. 'Believe me, I know.'

'I'm not Clare,' Fiona said defensively. 'You can't compare us.' She gave Jonathan a wistful smile. 'Maybe I'm pregnant now.'

'Fat chance,' Jonathan said grimly. 'About one in a million, to be precise. I don't think you have anything to worry about.' He stood up. 'Besides, it's obvious what you want. Don't you think I've been watching you at the hospital—how you react to babies? One day you'd look at me and I'd see the same accusing look that Clare gave me.' His voice cracked. 'I couldn't ever live through that again.'

Not looking at Fiona, Jonathan put his clothes back on. She was too upset to point out that they were still caked with plaster dust and he didn't seem to notice.

'Of course, I'm making assumptions here,' Jonathan said suddenly. 'Perhaps all you wanted was this.' He waved his hand towards the fire, seemingly wiping out their lovemaking with the dismissive gesture.

Fiona suddenly felt angry. Angry that he could denigrate the experience they had just shared—and even angrier that her choices were simply being removed.

'Perhaps it was,' she agreed coldly. Her previous rejection by him might have been only in her imagination, but this was real. And it was in the wake of her having just offered herself, body and soul, for the first time in her life. It was unbearable.

Jonathan's movements were jerky as he finished dressing. He, too, looked angry.

'Well, I'm sorry I can't oblige, in that case,' he responded. 'It means a little more to me than that.'

'And yet you could believe it doesn't for me?' Fiona's voice rose. She felt the prickle of tears behind her eyes.

'I couldn't say.' Jonathan picked up his coat. 'What I can say is this just isn't going to work.' He turned to look directly at Fiona, seemingly oblivious to the tears she could no longer check.

'I have commitments I'll have to honour here,' he said. 'But I'll see what arrangements can be made to cut my visit short. The worse this gets the harder it will be for both of us. Try to understand, please. And forgive me.'

With that he was gone. Fiona was left to cry on her own, and that was exactly what she did for some time. She didn't want to understand and she would never forgive him. He had given so much to her. That his love matched hers was obvious. But he had taken away even more. He had not, as he believed, given her the future she wanted. He had removed the only future she knew she needed. Their future. Their children. It felt like a mortal blow.

Finally, exhausted, Fiona went to bed. The roller coaster her emotions had been on that evening had settled into despair. Despair, heavily tinged with anger. She focused on the anger. It was easier to contemplate living with that than with the depths of despair.

CHAPTER SIX

FIONA knew Jon had seen her. The corridor was long but she had felt his gaze in her direction like a physical touch. The avoidance was deliberate. By the time she had turned from looking out of the window all she saw was Jon's back as he retraced his passage.

It was still raining this morning but the weather suited Fiona's mood. Sunshine would have been inappropriate. It also seemed fitting that she was assigned the gynaecological side of the on-call admissions. She would have felt out of sync with the vibrant rush and underlying excitement of the labour suite, and she didn't want to be reminded so vividly of last night's agonising.

The assumption that she, too, would one day experience the patient's side of the suite had always been there. It added to the thrill of a special delivery—sharing an intimate part of a couple's relationship, sensing the love and support, given as well as received, and watching the reverence with which a new life was welcomed.

It was the possibility that it wouldn't happen that made Fiona realise how strong her need was for that experience. But if she had it—it wouldn't be with Jonathan. And right now her need for him was also painfully strong. A choice was still there, she realised, but it was not one she felt willing to make, and Fiona felt angry at having it presented to her.

Even her first admission for the day appeared tailor-made. Mrs Pritchard had collapsed in a shop with excruciating abdominal pain, and had been transferred to hospital in an ambulance. Fiona's call had come from the general surgical registrar.

'You'll love her,' the registrar promised with a laugh. 'It'll take you a week just to go through her notes. There's three volumes of them, going back ten years. We've done every investigation we can think of—including surgical—and never managed to cure her for long. She's now complaining of irregular and unbearably painful periods so we thought it was only fair to give you lot a turn.'

'Perhaps the psychiatric team might be glad of a customer,' suggested Fiona.

'We tried that last time.' There was another chuckle from the surgical registrar. 'Problem is, she does come up with the odd genuine symptom—' A beep sounded in the background. 'Sorry, have to go. Have fun.'

Fiona's spirits sank still further when she drew back the curtains to greet her patient.

'I want a hysterectomy,' were Mrs Pritchard's first words. 'In fact, I must have one.'

'A hysterectomy is a major surgical procedure, Mrs Pritchard,' Fiona said firmly. 'Even with good indications, it's not something to be undertaken lightly. Like all major surgery, it has a significant risk of complications—some of them fatal.'

'I don't care.' Mrs Pritchard's voice rose. 'I'm quite convinced it's the only thing that will cure me. Oh-h!' With a spectacular groan Fiona's patient gripped the sheet with both hands and began to writhe about on the bed.

Fiona sighed heavily. She poked her head out of the curtain and caught the eye of a staff nurse.

'Could I have your assistance here for a few minutes, please, Louise?'

The 'few minutes' were extended considerably, but the staff nurse escaped long before Fiona. She kept hoping her beeper would sound, to indicate the arrival of a genuine emergency but, true to the day's form, it looked like being quiet.

Fiona finally withdrew, somewhat dazed, and headed automatically for the labour suite kitchen to find coffee. Then she hesitated, not wanting to find herself alone with Jonathan. She was standing undecided outside the door when Martin joined her and ushered her in. Jonathan was, indeed, in the room, Fiona noticed with dismay. He leaned comfortably against the window frame, a steaming mug in his hands. His eyes locked with Fiona's as she entered, but Martin seemed unaware of the tension between his companions.

'Three deliveries already,' Martin said happily. 'We're flat out. How are things upstairs?'

'Unusual,' Fiona conceded. She had to clear her throat to cover the effort it took to break the eye contact with Jonathan. 'I have a patient who would like a hysterectomy. Before lunch, if that's OK.'

'I'm sure we could fit it in,' Martin smiled. 'Don't you think, Jon?'

Jonathan's intense gaze hadn't left Fiona. His voice, however, was calm. 'What are the indications?'

'None that I can find.' Fiona directed her reply towards Martin. 'Unless it's the final trophy to add to her extensive medical history.'

'Even better.' Martin was spooning coffee into the

mugs. 'Let me guess. She's somewhere around fifty, never married, lives alone, probably a history of depression, has an impressive medical history but nothing startling—'

Fiona had to laugh. 'You've already met her.'

'No. And I don't think I want to. Send her back to her GP.'

'She doesn't have one. Having been through five in as many years, she can't find one that suits.'

'Pass her on to general surgery or the psych boys.' Jonathan straightened his tall frame and stretched his back.

'Been there, done that.' Fiona's voice tightened a little as Jonathan moved closer. She sipped her coffee quickly.

'Send her home, then.'

'But what if there really is something genuine that everybody's missed?' Fiona challenged. 'Maybe the wolf's really there this time.'

'What does your instinct tell you?' Now Jonathan was really close. His voice was soft and Fiona struggled with the sensations produced in her body. Her reply was husky.

'That it's not.'

'That's good enough for me,' Jonathan said quietly. Then his voice rose. 'But I'll have a look at her later, if you like. Better yet, why don't you go and see her, Martin?'

Jonathan stepped away to rinse his mug, and Fiona was shocked to realise she had completely forgotten Martin's presence in the room.

'I might just do that.' Martin sounded embarrassed, as though he'd suddenly realised how shut out he had been. 'If I feel strong enough.'

Fiona returned to the ward after her coffee. The depressing effect of her time with Mrs Pritchard had faded, but it returned with a rush as she passed the door of Doris Sinclair's private room. Strictly speaking, Doris was now the responsibility of the oncology team, but Fiona hesitated in the corridor, having seen Doris with her head in her hands sobbing uncontrollably.

Fiona closed her eyes briefly, only too aware of the depth of suffering she had glimpsed. It certainly served to put her own misery into perspective. She turned and entered Mrs Sinclair's room, closing the door quietly behind her.

For some time she just sat on the edge of the bed, her arms around the older woman, waiting for her grief to subside.

'I've decided against any further treatment,' Mrs Sinclair finally whispered.

Fiona passed her a box of tissues, and Doris blew her nose. 'That cancer specialist I saw this morning said it might not make any difference to what time I've got and could destroy the quality of what's left.'

Fiona nodded her understanding.

'The worst thing is...' Doris took a breath that was more of a sob '...my daughter is pregnant. It's my first grandchild and...and I may not see it. It'll never even know I existed.'

The tears flowed again and Fiona blinked back her own tears. She took Doris's hand and held it. They sat without speaking for several minutes, then Fiona cleared away the lump in her throat.

'My grandmother died when I was four,' she said softly, 'but I've never forgotten her because of something she once said.'

'What was that?' Doris spoke in a muffled voice as she reached for more tissues.

'I was struggling to do something—my buttons, I think—and she told me to just do my best. She said that as long as I truly knew I'd done my best, then it was all anyone could expect and it was good enough. But if I knew I wasn't truly doing my best then I'd have to try harder. Even now, when I'm trying something difficult, I can hear Gran's voice saying, "Just do your best", and I always wonder if I really am.' Fiona laughed. 'I usually end up trying a bit harder.'

Doris smiled weakly. 'At least you have that memory. I can't even give that to my grandchild.'

'You could, you know,' Fiona said thoughtfully.

Doris gave her a despairing glance and shook her head.

'You could give your grandchild a lot more than my gran gave me,' Fiona insisted gently, 'Why don't you write things down—maybe make a little scrapbook. Tell her—or him—about yourself and your life. Put in lots of photos and stories you remember from your own childhood. I would love to have known more about my grandmother. Your daughter can keep it until he or she's old enough.'

Fiona paused, unsure whether she could detect any interest in her idea. 'Put in the bits of advice that all your years of experience have given you. I think your daughter, as much as any grandchildren, would treasure it.'

Fiona's beeper sounded and she had to excuse herself. She left Doris at least looking calmer, and Fiona found that remembering her grandmother's maxim had given her strength of her own. She just had to remind herself to do her best.

Fiona deliberately liaised with Martin over the next couple of days, trying to reduce her contact with Jonathan. For his part, Jonathan also seemed to be doing his best to stay away and to get his commitments over and done with, busily preparing lectures and organising demonstrations. Despite their attempts to control their working environment, however, they seemed to be constantly thrown together.

It came to a head on Thursday afternoon. There had really been no reason for Jonathan to stand breathing over her shoulder during the final moments of Mary Jennings's delivery. Mary was a first-time, enthusiastic mother-to-be, and the labour had been fast but uncomplicated.

'Stop pushing, Mary,' Fiona instructed. 'Just pant for a minute.'

'You'll have to do an episiotomy,' Jonathan advised quietly in her ear. 'She's going to tear.'

'No more pushing, Mary,' Fiona said more firmly. But Mary was uncooperative.

'I can't,' she gasped.

Fiona reached for the scissors a split second before Jonathan, and his hand closed over hers. Startled, she jerked her hand away at the same time he released hers. The scissors clattered to the floor under the astonished gaze of the midwife, Catherine, who recovered quickly and rushed to supply a clean pair. But it was too late. Mary's final, determined push had delivered the baby's head and the delivery was completed swiftly. Catherine cleaned out the baby's nose and mouth and placed him in Mary's arms. Fiona injected the oxytocin to speed up delivery of the placenta and surveyed the damage. The jagged tear in the perineal tissue was going to take some time to repair. She moved to the basin to rescrub.

'That was unnecessary,' Jonathan admonished as he finished washing his hands.

'Yes, it was,' Fiona agreed sharply.

'Next time, perhaps you can anticipate the possible uncooperative behaviour of your patient and move in a little faster.'

'Next time, perhaps I won't have to deal with unnecessary distractions.'

'I think it was a case of clumsiness.' Jonathan's voice was angry, but still quiet enough to be covered by the sound of the running water.

'I think it was a case of unwarranted interference,' Fiona hissed in return.

They glared at each other. Jonathan threw his hand towel into the linen basket. 'I have a lecture to prepare. I'll leave you to your suturing. Without interference.'

The lecture was on Friday, and Fiona belatedly joined the lunchtime crowd that packed the seminar room.

Standing just inside the doorway, behind a couple of other latecomers, Fiona had a clear view of Jon's profile and a not very adequate view of the slide projection screen. Her field of vision most comfortably included the front row of the audience, prominent among them being Doreen Roberts. Doreen had her gaze fixed on the speaker and appeared to find the topic riveting.

Certainly the history of, and potential for, gynaecological endoscopy was fascinating, but Fiona had to wonder why it would be particularly gripping for a paediatric consultant. She smiled inwardly, without mirth. She knew precisely why it was gripping. And, who knew, maybe it would be reciprocated. Doreen was far too involved in her career to be interested in having children—it could be an ideal match.

Fiona noted Doreen's rather short skirt, her legs crossed in a confident, almost languid manner. She had an unreadable expression on her face that, Fiona decided somewhat waspishly, looked smug. She traced the line of Dr Roberts's intense gaze back to the speaker, realising she had largely missed about thirty years of the history of diagnostic laparoscopy.

Jon rapidly went through a series of slides, discussing laser surgical instruments and their application, then embarked on an overall view of the types of surgery now possible through laparoscopic techniques. Fiona found the words flowed over her as she listened to the sound of his voice, whilst watching the smooth movement of his body and hands.

He looked perfectly at ease in this situation, and Fiona imagined he would be exactly the same in front of hundreds of his colleagues at an international symposium. It was no wonder his career had advanced as far as it had. And would now continue to do so when he returned overseas.

Fiona felt her anger at Jonathan resurface, and knew she would remember nothing of the future possibilities for endoscopic surgery. She glared at Doreen Roberts for finding Jonathan attractive and assuming he was available, and then she glared at Jonathan for being both so attractive and unavailable to herself.

As if he'd felt the heat of her gaze, Jonathan turned his head and caught her eye. His speech did not falter but a frown creased his forehead momentarily, as though he was aware of a threatened interruption.

Fiona felt a flush of colour on her face, transferred her gaze and found that Doreen Roberts was now staring at her. The smug expression seemed surprised, even irritated. Fiona felt her colour rise further and slipped out through the open doorway.

As she marched back up towards the ward Fiona dodged orderlies pushing patients in wheelchairs and on trolleys, kitchen staff pushing cumbersome meal trolleys, and the lunch-hour traffic of staff returning from the cafeteria. Someone said hello but Fiona didn't notice. She felt at odds with the whole environment, and angry with herself for her reaction.

She was behaving like a teenager, she told herself irately. She had to snap out of it—get on with both her career and her life. At least with a weekend on call, she would have little time to sit around and brood.

Fiona made a determined effort to avoid Jonathan, which worked well for the first part of the weekend duty. Admissions were steady but uncomplicated, and Fiona found time to spend an enjoyable half-hour chatting to Shirley Cook and admiring her son. At four and a half pounds, he had needed only a couple of days' monitoring in the neonatal unit, and now they were back on the ward and already talking about going home.

By Saturday afternoon Fiona felt confident when she picked up the phone in the labour suite office to call Martin. When he failed to answer his beeper she replaced the receiver and drummed her fingertips on the desk top.

'Need some help?'

Fiona jumped at the sound of Jonathan's voice. 'No. I—that is, I was trying to call Martin.'

'He's tied up in Theatre for a while,' Jonathan said calmly. 'I've just left him to finish up a Caesar.'

'Oh.' Fiona knew she sounded irritated. 'Well, it's not really urgent. I just wanted to discuss an admission.'

'Perhaps I can hclp.' Jonathan's tone was measured, carefully professional, it seemed to Fiona. 'We are on the same team, you know.'

'Are we?' Fiona couldn't help the reply that sprang to her lips. The spat that had followed Mary Jennings's delivery still rankled. Fiona knew he had been right and was angry with herself. Jonathan's silent gaze was unreadable and Fiona shrugged slightly.

'I've just admitted a thirty-one-year-old woman, Janet Redbury. She's twenty-three weeks pregnant and came in because of slight bleeding and minimal contractions. She lost a baby two years ago at the same stage for no obvious cause.'

Jonathan nodded.

'Her cervix is effaced and dilated, membranes bulging but intact, and there's no clinical suggestion of any infection.'

'And the query?' Jonathan seemed to be waiting for Fiona's opinion.

'If she delivers at this stage she will probably lose the baby.'

Jonathan nodded again.

'The signs of labour aren't pronounced. Contractions are widely spaced and weak and there's no significant blood loss.' Fiona warmed to her topic, suddenly finding it easy to talk to Jonathan. 'I'm wondering if this is a case of true cervical incompetence and whether an emergency cervical cerclage at this point could make a difference.'

Martin, still dressed in theatre gear, had come into the office. He looked interested.

'Cervical suture as treatment for pre-term labour?' He raised his eyebrows theatrically.

'In this case, quite possibly,' Jonathan agreed. 'If Fiona's right, she fits the criteria where the technique is considered to be of value.'

'I don't believe I'm incorrect,' Fiona said stiffly.

'Oh, I'm not questioning your clinical judgement,' Jonathan said soothingly. 'It's just that the situation could change dramatically. We'll observe her for twelve hours and if nothing changes we'll go ahead.'

'What gestation?' Martin enquired.

'Twenty-three weeks,' Fiona told him. 'Even a delay of just a few weeks could mean a huge difference in prognosis.'

Martin looked doubtful. 'Could be a long shot.'

'It's worth a try,' Fiona said defensively. 'They lost their first baby at this stage and they're terrified of it happening again. I think we should do whatever we can.'

'Of course.' Jonathan sounded reassuring. 'We will.'

'I've never done one,' Martin said. 'What's the technique?'

'Multiple-bite McDonald-type suture with Mersilene tape.' Jonathan leaned back against the desk. 'Either using regional or general anaesthesia. Membranes can be pushed back with the inflated balloon of a urinary catheter or, if necessary, the amount of fluid can be reduced with transabdominal amniocentesis. We give prophylactic IV antibiotics and ritodrine, then keep our fingers crossed.'

'I hope it works,' Fiona breathed fervently.

'I'll come and see Mrs Redbury now,' Jonathan said, 'and have a chat to her. But we can't raise her hopes too much just yet.'

'Anything you'd like done upstairs, Fiona?' asked Martin. 'You can do the next delivery, if you like.'

'OK.' Fiona pondered and then smiled. 'I know. You can evaluate Mrs Pritchard for discharge. Nobody's been near her for a couple of days and she wants to know her results.'

'We're all too scared to go near her,' Martin sighed. 'I thought you were going to send her home yesterday.'

'I was,' Fiona said vaguely. 'I got tied up.'

'I know!' Martin snapped his fingers. 'We'll keep her in till next week. Aren't you looking for a patient for your demonstration laparoscopic hysterectomy, Jon?'

Martin left while they were still laughing. Fiona and Jonathan were alone again, and their gazes caught and held. There was a long moment of silence.

'Fiona... I...' Jon's eyes held a look of pain that cut into Fiona.

She took a deep breath. Their professional discussion had been easy, even enjoyable, but now the atmosphere had changed with remarkable rapidity into one of unbearable tension. It would be so easy to simply close the gap between them and throw herself into his arms. Clearly, he wanted it as much as she did. So easy—and so impossibly difficult. She let out her breath slowly.

'Let's go and see Mrs Redbury, shall we?'

The evening dragged on with a lengthy delivery, and it was nearly midnight before Fiona could take an incomplete miscarriage up to Theatre for a D and C, which she performed on her own. Having finished the procedure, she curled up wearily in a comfortable chair in the theatre staffroom and was almost asleep when she felt a light touch on her knee. Looking up, she found Jon crouched in front of her, his eyes level with her own.

'Are you OK, Pen?'

Tears sprang to Fiona's eyes at his tone and the use of her nickname—something he had avoided for days. Jon drew her to him and gently wiped away her tears.

'I'm sorry, Pen,' he said quietly. 'Hurting you is the last thing in the world I want to do.'

'You're hurting yourself just as much,' Fiona said brokenly. 'Can't you see that?'

Jonathan nodded. Then he stood up slowly. 'At least I can give you the chance to get over it quickly, Pen,' he said softly. 'You'll understand one day when you have your own family—your own children. You'll thank me then.'

'Don't count on it,' Fiona snapped. She uncurled her legs and scrambled to her feet. 'And don't treat me like a child. My name's Fiona.'

She walked out on him, hating herself for doing so and desperately wanting to go back and beg him to change his mind. Somehow they could work it out. But pride and anger mingled with her exhaustion and she felt too overwhelmed to even think any more.

The rest of the weekend call passed in a blur. They took Janet Redbury to Theatre on Sunday afternoon. The contractions had responded to medication and virtually stopped, the dilation had remained static and the membranes were still intact. There had been no evidence of infection. Jonathan did the procedure himself, with both Martin and Fiona as interested observers. There were no complications and Fiona shared Janet Redbury's excitement at the renewed prospect of a successful outcome to her pregnancy.

Fiona's role of observing Jonathan seemed to continue for much of the next week as his demonstration surgical sessions finally got under way. Even Martin joined her in watching the surgery on video relay as the other Obs & Gynae consultants were keen to be present and assist.

The techniques were fascinating but struck Fiona as being almost robotic. The instruments, able to cut, suture and control bleeding, were all introduced through tiny portholes and controlled by a surgeon, guided by images on a monitor. The procedures took longer than conventional surgery and appeared awkward at times.

Fiona decided she had no desire to incorporate the skills needed into her own career, but she could see Martin was gripped by the possibilities. As one long session ended she smiled at the senior registrar.

'Great new toys, eh?'

'You said it.' Martin's eyes shone. 'I'd love to have a go myself.'

'Any word from Edinburgh?'

'No. But have you heard about Jack Owens?'

'No.' Fiona had barely given the absent consultant any thought at all in the last few weeks. 'What about him?'

'Apparently, he and his family have fallen in love with Wales. They're planning to make it a permanent arrangement.'

'Is there a job there?'

'Not at the Royal, but there may be a position coming up somewhere not far off.'

'That means they'll have to replace him here.' For a wild moment Fiona thought of what it could mean to have Jonathan permanently in Christchurch. Then she saw hope lighting Martin's face.

'Exactly. Guess who might have a very good chance of landing the job?'

'I hope you do, Martin,' Fiona said warmly. 'You'd be great.' As if Jonathan Fletcher would tear himself away from the wonderful facilities and opportunities which had helped create his international reputation to settle in what must now seem like the back of beyond. Unless, of course, the attractions of a certain paediatric consultant were making themselves felt. She wanted to change the subject. 'How's Lisa?'

Martin laughed. 'I've definitely landed *that* job. Things couldn't be better. We're going out tomorrow night to see if our luck extends to some success at the casino.' He looked thoughtfully at Fiona. 'Why don't you come with us?'

'What—and play gooseberry?' Fiona laughed. 'No, thanks.'

'I happen to know somebody who would be over the moon at the prospect of a date with you.' Martin looked as though he expected a firm rebuff. 'Tony Lloyd, in A and E. He's a good friend of mine—will be my best man, in fact.'

'Hmm.' Fiona had met Tony. About Fiona's height, thin and blond, he had struck her as a pleasant though not particularly exciting acquaintance.

'We're going black tie, just for fun,' Martin added.

'Well, that settles it. I haven't anything to wear so I couldn't possibly go.' Fiona cast an idle glance back towards the video monitor as the observation room emptied of spectators. Theatre staff were cleaning up, laughing and chatting. In the background she could see Jonathan removing his mask, also laughing. His companion's mask was removed and Fiona's eyes widened.

She and Martin had been watching the surgery secondhand because of numbers while Doreen Roberts had been observing in the theatre itself. She turned back to Martin.

'On second thoughts, Martin, a night out might just do me good. I'd love to come.'

Fiona made a flying visit to the ward, before leaving the hospital that evening. Janet Redbury did not need any medical attention, but the daily check and chat had become part of the routine. Long-stay patients were unusual and the women had established a friendship quite apart from their professional relationship. Fiona found Janet feeling well but very bored with her confinement.

'I've never been in bed this long in my life,' she complained. 'I'm sick of reading and television and I've got little knitted things coming out of my ears.'

Fiona laughed. 'You need something a bit different to distract you.'

'Like going home?'

'No way. Sorry. This is the best place for you both right now.'

'I know.' Janet sighed heavily. 'I've just got too much time to think—and worry about things.'

'Be positive,' Fiona said firmly. 'I have a good feeling about this. Why don't you do something for the baby that isn't knitting?'

'Like what?'

Fiona thought of the suggestion she had given Doris Sinclair. Doris had now been discharged but she had asked to see Fiona before she left. With quiet enthusiasm Doris had told her of the plans she had for her scrapbook and had thanked Fiona for the idea.

'I feel like I've got something positive to focus on,' she had said. 'It's the best thing anyone could have given me.'

Now Fiona eyed Janet thoughtfully. 'How much do you know about your grandparents?'

Janet looked astonished. 'Bits and pieces. I've got some photos. Why?'

'Why not make a scrapbook? A sort of extended family tree. Some history for the baby.'

'Hmm.' Janet considered the idea. 'I could ask Mum and Dad, I suppose. It would give us something to talk about when they come to visit.'

'Might be interesting for you, too. At least it would be a change. Delve into the past instead of dwelling so much on the future. Speaking of which…' Fiona glanced at her watch '…I've got to go. Big night tonight.'

'Lucky you,' sighed Janet. 'Have fun.'

'Oh, I intend to,' Fiona said decisively. 'See you tomorrow.'

Lack of anything suitable to wear presented Fiona with a challenge she was in the mood to overcome. The style of dress was not a problem in the exclusive boutique she chose. A slim-fitting sheath with shoestring straps, the dress was appropriate and astonishingly elegant. Fiona was pleasantly surprised at how sophisticated it made her feel.

The colour was more of a problem. The shop assistant encouraged her to be daring, with either scarlet or emerald-green, but Fiona wanted to explore the sensation of sophistication further.

'I'll stick to black, please.'

'Of course.' The assistant looked resigned. 'Might I suggest a jacket and shoes as accessories?'

'Why not?' Fiona agreed. 'And you might know of a hairdresser near here as well. I'd like to do something a bit different with my hair for once.'

The casino was a new multi-million-dollar venture that had as much attraction for the tourists and curious locals as the dedicated gambler. The whole idea of the establishment and the opulence of the exterior and entranceway had been offputting to Fiona, but trying something completely different was certainly a distraction from the low mood she had been in for the last two weeks.

Martin and Tony looked elegant in their evening suits, and Lisa contributed to their admiring comments of Fiona when she joined them.

The group had dinner before exploring the gaming halls, and Fiona found her spirits lifting as the evening progressed. Martin was, as usual, entertaining company. Lisa's vivacity encouraged him and Tony showed himself to possess a keen wit. Fiona allowed herself to be drawn into an amusing commentary on the potential gambling habits of the crowd of people they were observing.

'Now, there's a compulsive gambler if ever I saw one.' Martin was grinning broadly.

Lisa followed his gaze. 'Why, that's Philip Reece, isn't it?'

Startled, Fiona looked around. She hadn't expected to meet anyone they knew but, sure enough, Philip Reece and his wife stood at the next table. They appeared to be watching rather than gambling. A shout went up from the group around the table and a pile of chips was pushed towards the winner. Fiona kept staring as she realised she also knew the winner. Doreen Roberts. With a sinking sensation she looked further, knowing who her partner for the evening was likely to be. Jonathan saw her at the same time, looked disconcerted but then moved purposefully towards their group.

'Fancy meeting you here.' Jonathan nodded at Martin. 'I was told I couldn't miss seeing the city's latest attraction, but I hadn't picked my staff as gamblers.'

Martin introduced Lisa and Tony, but Jonathan's eyes kept straying back to Fiona. He waited until Martin was introducing his companions to the Reeces and Doreen Roberts, who had joined them.

'You look stunning, Pen.' He slowly let his gaze travel over her hair, which the hairdresser had cleverly twisted to form a roll at the sides with the length neatly coiled into a knot at the back, over her bare shoulders and down the length of the slim-fitting black dress.

His look was virtually a caress, and Fiona took a certain satisfaction in seeing Doreen observing both his attention and her appearance. Her expression suggested that perhaps, for the first time, she viewed Fiona as competition. Fiona decided the exorbitant cost of the dress had been worth it.

'You don't look so bad yourself,' Fiona returned lightly. She wanted to laugh inwardly at the understatement she was making, but it was too painful. The sight of Jonathan Fletcher in full evening dress had been disconcerting, to say the least. She wondered if

Doreen Roberts had had the opportunity to find out that the body beneath was just as magnificent.

'I'm off to Auckland in the morning,' Jonathan said brightly. 'Any messages for Daniel?'

'Tell him to answer my letter,' Fiona replied. 'Or at least ring me some time.'

'I'll be up there all next week as well.' Jonathan included Martin in his comment. 'Philip has kindly agreed to cover me so I can talk to the interested parties up there.'

'He's a popular man,' Philip Reece put in. 'We'll have to try and keep him here a bit longer at this rate.'

'Definitely.' Doreen Roberts smiled at Jonathan. She glanced pointedly at Fiona and then towards Tony.

Jonathan's gaze followed the same pattern, but then returned to Fiona. 'I must go. Early flight tomorrow. Have a good evening.' With another quick glance at Tony, Jonathan gave an approving smile and nod.

As though sensing that Fiona's pleasure from the outing had dissipated, her group also curtailed their evening not long afterwards. Fiona declined Tony's offer of a drink somewhere else and went home alone. She was obviously doomed to fail in distracting herself from her personal turmoil so she might as well sit and brood for a while.

A good cry was probably justified as well at this point. But after that she would need to pull herself together and work out a strategy to get through the weekend and the next week. With a bit of luck she might hit upon a solution to see her through until

Jonathan Fletcher removed himself from her life again.

She had no intention of trying to see any further into the future than that.

CHAPTER SEVEN

PLANNING a strategy and putting it into practice were two quite different matters. What sounded admirable and feasible in theory could fall apart so easily when put to a practical test.

The new day and the new plan had started well for Fiona. Rising early, she had retraced the route she had taken Jonathan on so recently. Saddling the spirited grey mare, Fiona had ridden long and hard, away from the river and right up into the hills, as fast as reasonable safety limits permitted. The mare had revelled in the challenge.

Fiona had been exhilarated but poor Belle collapsed in offended exhaustion as the ride ended and Fiona groomed the horse. Too tired even for her customary dip in the water trough, the old dog climbed wearily into the back seat of the car and fell asleep, refusing to get out when they arrived home at the cottage.

Fiona showered, changed her jodhpurs for jeans, then drove to the hospital with Belle still asleep in the back seat. Finding a shady place to park, she reached over and stroked a soft black ear.

'Won't be long,' she promised.

She collected a Dictaphone and a pile of patient case notes, Fiona found a quiet spot and spent the next two hours catching up on a backlog of patient discharge summaries. It was a tedious job.

The medical and nursing notes had to be reread to

remind her of any complications during an admission, then a summary was compiled of history, presenting complaint, investigations and treatment given in hospital, drugs or recommendations given on discharge and what follow-up had been arranged—with either outpatient appointments, further investigations or referral back to a GP.

Mrs Pritchard's discharge summary was the last and most onerous. Fiona finally hit the home stretch with a sigh of relief.

'Due to Mrs Pritchard's vagueness regarding the nature of the irregularity of her cycles, she has been advised to keep a detailed diary of her cycle days and symptoms. We will review her at Outpatients in three months, or earlier if an acute problem arises.'

Fiona chewed her lip, then ran the tape back and listened until she heard the words 'three months'. She depressed the button and erased the final comment. Why invite trouble? she thought. Besides, as far as she knew, there was no GP to whom to send a copy of the summary.

Putting the tapes on top of the pile of case notes, Fiona left them on the departmental secretary's desk. Someone would be delighted to find them first thing on Monday morning, she thought with a grin.

The task satisfyingly completed, Fiona moved straight on to the next part of her strategy—spending time with her family. Belle was overjoyed to see the children and Laura welcomed Fiona with a hug.

'About time we saw you, Fee. We've finished lunch, I'm afraid, but I'll make you a sandwich.'

'That'd be great but I can make it.' Fiona bent to kiss Jennifer, drowsing in her pram, and tousled

Michael's hair. The walk to the kitchen was difficult, with the toddler hanging grimly on to her leg.

'Let go of Fee's leg,' ordered Jack. The twins stopped romping with Belle, who gratefully slunk up into an armchair to continue her recuperation.

'Belle's getting old,' Laura commented sadly. 'She looks like she needs a rocking chair.'

'She had a hard morning.' Fiona smiled. 'And loved every minute of it.'

Alan was finishing the lunch dishes. He welcomed Fiona enthusiastically, but with the same subtle reproach as his wife.

'What have you been up to? A quick trip to Europe and back?'

'This and that.' Fiona laughed as she rummaged in the cupboard and fridge. 'Work mostly.'

The twins had decided to supervise the sandwich-making and sat on the edge of the kitchen table, swinging their legs.

'Put peanut butter in,' directed Jack. 'Lots and lots.'

'And jam,' added Sarah.

'I like Marmite.' Jack changed his mind. 'With cheese.'

'Mushed-up eggs,' giggled Sarah. 'With those little green bits.'

'Shall I just put a bit of everything in and save the hard work of deciding?' suggested Fiona.

The twins thought this was hilarious and erupted into shrieks of laughter.

Fiona glanced at Alan. 'Oh, I stripped all the wallpaper off my living room, as well as working. Thought I'd improve the place a bit.'

'Good idea.'

'Well, actually, I've made it look a lot worse. I rather wish I hadn't started. I'm not sure what to do next.'

'I'll come and have a look tomorrow,' offered Alan. 'We'll make a list of the things you'll need.'

Laura nodded. 'If you get everything during the week we'll come over next weekend and give you a hand.'

'I'd really appreciate that,' Fiona said gratefully. 'If I don't get a kick-start it might stay looking awful for ever.' She didn't add that getting on with her re-decoration was also part of her coping strategy. She had no intention of discussing or even thinking about Jonathan Fletcher today if she could help it.

The twins eyed the cheese and tomato sandwich Fiona was making with disappointment.

'Jack's got a girlfriend,' Sarah told Fiona importantly.

Fiona looked up and grinned at Jack, who looked suitably embarrassed.

'Have you, Jack? What's her name?'

'Nicola.' Sarah answered for him. 'They hold hands and stuff.'

'She must be nice.' Fiona bit hungrily into her sandwich and smiled at Laura, who set a cup of coffee in front of her.

Alan came into the kitchen, carrying Jennifer. He handed the baby to Laura.

'She thinks it's about time for her lunch.'

'Jack's going to marry Nicola,' Sarah stated.

'I am not!' contradicted Jack.

'You are, too. You said so.' Sarah's voice rose indignantly and Laura raised an eyebrow in her daughter's direction.

'OK,' Jack conceded. 'I guess I will.'

'You don't have to decide right now,' Fiona said with a smile.

'Oh, I want to,' Jack said. 'Nicola's into rockets too.'

'Just as well.' Fiona managed to keep her face appropriately serious.

'They're going to get married and have lots and lots of children,' added Sarah happily.

Fiona put down her sandwich. 'People don't get married just to have children, you know.'

Sarah looked astonished, both at Fiona's statement and her tone of voice. 'Why not?'

'Some people might not want to have children,' Fiona answered more calmly. 'And some people can't have them.'

The twins eyed each other with disbelief.

'Why not?' echoed Jack.

Fiona looked at the wide eyes confronting her and wished she hadn't begun the discussion. Laura came to her rescue.

'Why don't you get Dad to put *Cinderella* on the video for you?'

'Cool!' Both twins scrambled off the table and herded their father out of the kitchen.

Laura settled the baby more comfortably at her breast.

'What's up, Fee?'

'*Is* having children the be all and end all of marriage?' Fiona's tone was defensive.

'Of course not. But it's a very important part for a lot of people. From the kids' perspective it must certainly come tops, don't you think? I thought you were dead keen on having your own little tribe in the not too distant future.'

'Oh, I am,' Fiona murmured. 'It's just...' Her voice trailed off into silence. She fiddled with the crust of her sandwich.

'Has this got anything to do with Jon?' Laura glanced speculatively at her sister.

'What on earth makes you say that?' Fiona avoided the glance.

'Jon might not have known how you used to feel about him,' Laura said carefully, 'but it was pretty obvious to me. Understandable, too. If Alan hadn't already been on the scene I might well have fallen for him myself. It was a shame you weren't just a few years older.' Laura transferred Jennifer to her other breast. 'You were pretty rattled that night he turned up here and we haven't seen much of you since. And now you seem to have rather a lot on your mind. Does it all add up, Fee? Is it really still ancient history?'

'I thought it was. In fact, I was sure of it.' Fiona sighed heavily. 'I guess I was wrong.'

'And is Jon now aware of how you feel?'

Fiona nodded. With a wistful smile she added, 'I think he feels the same way.'

Laura frowned at Fiona's odd tone but then smiled encouragingly. 'He's not married any more.'

'No,' agreed her sister. 'And if he ever does get married again it won't be to me.'

'Why ever not?' Laura shifted the now-drowsing Jennifer to her shoulder and began to rub the baby's back.

'As far as he's concerned, a marriage without children is not good enough.'

'So what's the problem? I haven't noticed any aversion to babies on your part,' Laura said with a grin.

'Jonathan's marriage to Clare broke up because it turned out he's unable to have children. She resented it being his fault and ended up getting pregnant by someone else.'

'Oh, no!' Laura was horrified. 'I had no idea. And how do you feel—about the idea of not having children?'

'I don't know,' Fiona replied heavily. 'It's not really much of a choice, is it? The man I love or the family I want. Any solution would be a compromise.' She looked at Laura despairingly. 'I'm not sure I want to live with a compromise for the rest of my life.'

'There's always adoption.'

Fiona shook her head. 'He's already been through all the options and has no intention of ever doing it again. He's a very determined man, our Jonathan. He's made up his mind and will stick to it, no matter how much it hurts us both.'

'I suppose he had to be that strong to get through life as well as he has. In a way, I can understand why he's so obsessed with the idea of family.'

'Oh, so can I,' Fiona agreed. 'Of course I can. But is it a good enough reason to throw away something that, for the present, seems as good as it could ever get?'

'Things must have progressed a lot in the last few weeks.'

'Mmm.' Fiona felt herself colouring. The sisters looked at each other silently and were both smiling when Alan came back into the kitchen.

'What am I missing?' he enquired. 'Something very interesting, by the look of it.'

'Woman talk,' Laura told him briskly. She winked at Fiona. 'We'll continue this discussion some other time.'

Alan came around to the cottage the next morning, and Fiona found herself writing a long list of supplies and gathering technical hints for her redecoration. Sandpaper, filler and polyurethane for the window frames, scrapers, paint and rollers for the ceiling, more filler, size, glue and wallpaper for the walls.

'Don't worry about the ladders and trestles,' Alan said. 'We'll bring those.'

Then it was a trip to the hardware shop, and Fiona spent the entire afternoon happily choosing paint and paper and collecting all the other materials, as well as a lot more advice. Returning to the cottage, she emptied the living room. She wedged the desk into her bedroom and loaded the top with boxes of books, then manhandled the couch out into the garage.

After a hurried dinner Fiona fished out the sand-paper and blocks she had purchased, and spent the evening attacking the window frames. All in all, it was a productive and satisfying day, and by the time Fiona went to bed she was congratulating herself on how well her strategy was working.

The week at work passed surprisingly quickly. The emotional strain was gone to a large extent, with Jonathan away in Auckland, but a lot of the excite-ment was also gone. Even while she had dreaded their encounters, she knew she had waited and hoped for them. The thumping heartbeat, the almost painful tingles of desire might have been disturbing, but without them life seemed very flat. Even the most interesting cases of the week had a mechanical feel about them.

The bright spots during the week were the daily visits to Janet Redbury. Fiona's idea of a scrapbook had again taken root and Janet's bed was usually littered with old photographs, letters and mementos that her relatives were providing.

'I don't know where to begin,' she groaned. 'Look—here's a photo of my great-aunt Daisy. I didn't even know I *had* a great-aunt Daisy.'

'It's a pretty name.' Fiona peered at the faded sepia photograph.

'It is, isn't it? I think I'll call the baby Daisy. I suppose I'd better hope for a girl,' Janet added as an afterthought.

They both laughed. 'Well, she'll want to know who she's named after, then,' Fiona said. 'You'd better get sorting.'

On Wednesday, however, a familiar rush of excitement flooded through Fiona when she arrived on the ward to find a large bunch of flowers waiting for her. The ward staff and Martin Cox were all grinning broadly as she eagerly fumbled to open the tiny envelope containing the card.

'*No winnings, but still a lucky night for me.*'

Fiona frowned at the card, trying to make sense of the message. Jonathan had been at the casino with Doreen, so why was she getting the roses?

The staff nurse was humming the 'Wedding March'. Martin peered over her shoulder at the card.

'He said he was going to send some. I told him pink was your favourite colour.'

'Who?'

'Tony, of course. How many admirers do you keep up your sleeve at any one time?' Martin was watching Fiona closely and couldn't fail to register the level of disappointment his words evoked.

'Oh, heaps,' Fiona quipped lightly. She tucked the card back in its envelope and put it in her pocket. 'I'll leave them here in the office, Louise,' she told the staff nurse. 'That way more people can enjoy them. Besides...' she gave Martin a very direct look '...my favourite colour is yellow.'

Fiona knew she was being ungracious, but the complication of fending off a romantic approach by Tony was the last thing she wanted to contemplate at present. She had to make the message as clear as possible. With a bit of luck, it might filter back to Tony through Martin. Cowardly, she admitted, but preferable right now.

At home in the evenings Fiona applied herself with diligence and increasing skill to her redecoration. She filled the holes in the window frames, finished the sanding and polyurethaned the richly toned wood. She then spent many hours carefully plastering the damage to the walls which the enthusiastic stripping had exacerbated. She tried hard, but was not entirely successful in avoiding memories of the evening the damage had occurred.

By the time Laura, Alan and the children arrived on Saturday she was ready for the next stage. Alan set up the ladders and planks, and then he and Fiona began to scrape the peeling paint from the ceiling. Thanks to the small size of the room, this unpleasant task was completed by the time Laura returned with the children and Belle from their outing to the park.

She took them home with her after lunch while

Alan and Fiona worked on, painting the ceiling. Alan rolled the flat sections while Fiona used a small brush to go over the central rose and the cornices. She scrambled off her ladder repeatedly to wipe splashes off the newly finished window frames.

Her arms ached by the time they stopped to join Laura and the children for dinner, but the first coat of quick-drying paint looked so good when Fiona returned home that she stayed up until 2 a.m. putting the second coat on by herself.

Sunday was cold and wet, but the tiny cottage was so full of people and laughter that nobody paid any attention to the weather. The living room was filled with a large trestle table on which lengths of wallpaper were being cut and pasted. The twins and Michael were at the kitchen table, which was strewn with paint, paper, crayons and playdough. Jennifer slept peacefully in her pram in the corner, with Belle on guard at her wheels.

Fiona and Laura measured, cut and pasted the paper and then handed it to Alan, who eased it to hang correctly, before pressing it flat. Fiona had chosen a tiny floral pattern, and much debate was needed with every section of paper to ensure that the pattern was matching. They ordered pizzas to be delivered for lunch, and the twins raced excitedly to the door when the knock came. Whooping happily, they dragged a surprised Jonathan back with them to the living room.

'I think I've come at a bad time,' he said apologetically.

'You're part of this family,' Laura told him firmly. 'There's no such thing as a bad time.'

'The twins are more excited about you than the pizza,' Fiona observed with a grin. 'I hope you realise how honoured you are.' She avoided meeting his gaze. It was hard enough trying to ignore the messages her body was sending her without the intensity eye contact would have added.

'Pizza?' Jonathan looked confused. Another knock at the door sent the twins flying, and Fiona reached for her wallet.

'I hope you're hungry. We've ordered enough to feed an army.'

'He'll need the fuel.' Alan started down from his ladder. 'There's plenty of work here for the afternoon.'

Somehow they all fitted into the tiny kitchen, where a very noisy but enjoyable meal was consumed. Belle got far more than her usual share.

'I really dropped by to let you know how Daniel is and to pass on his love.' Jonathan accepted a second slice of pizza and shifted the blue playdough ball Sarah had placed on his plate.

'That's a cake,' Sarah informed him. 'You're supposed to eat it.'

'I'll save it for later,' Jonathan promised. 'It looks delicious.'

'How is Danny?' Laura removed the salami from Michael's pizza and gave it to Jack.

'Great. Shelley's pregnant again.' Jonathan caught Fiona's eye and Laura intercepted the glance.

'They don't know when to stop,' she said lightly. 'Almost as bad as us.'

'Probably be twins,' Alan laughed.

'No.' Laura shook her head decisively. 'It's only the women in the family that produce twins. It's been a tradition of six generations now. At least one set for every branch down the female side.'

'Why did it have to be us?' Alan groaned. He also removed a blue playdough cake from his plate. Then he grinned. 'I'm sure Fiona would have been delighted to oblige.'

There was a sudden silence. Alan looked disconcerted, as though wondering what he'd said to cause it. Michael broke the tension by turning his plate upside down and crowing with delight as Belle moved in to accept the generous offering.

'Come on, Jon.' Alan rose hurriedly from the table before another silence could fall. 'I need some expert help in there.'

'Expert! I've never hung a piece of wallpaper in my life.'

Jonathan looked relieved as he stood up. 'I have had a little practice at stripping, though.'

'Ooh! Do tell.' Laura giggled.

'I'm discussing wallpaper here.' Jonathan glanced at the grin Fiona couldn't suppress but her face sobered as she thought how near to the mark the innuendo had really come. Her eyes locked with his, the tension like a solid wall between them.

Aware of the undercurrent, Laura busied herself clearing the table. Sarah saved the moment from becoming even more awkward.

'Here.' She presented Jonathan with yet another small blue ball. 'You still haven't eaten your cake.'

'And you still haven't eaten your pizza,' Laura admonished Fiona as Jonathan escaped.

'I'm not that fussed about it,' Fiona admitted. 'I'll have something later.'

'How about some coffee, then?'

'Ugh, no, thanks. I'm off coffee today as well.'

Fiona looked questioningly at Laura's expression. 'What on earth is that look for?'

'I go off coffee myself. Every time.'

'Every time what?' Fiona was now smiling at her older sister, but Laura failed to return the smile.

'Every time I'm pregnant.'

There was a long moment of silence as Fiona absorbed her amazement. Then she frowned.

'If that's a joke, Laura, it's a really bad one.'

'Sorry.' Laura turned her attention to the dishes. 'I rang home last night,' she said brightly, in an obvious attempt to change the subject.

'How are they?' Fiona was relieved to follow the conversational lead.

'Mum's a bit worried about Dad. She thinks he might be getting some chest pain.'

Alan entered the kitchen, carrying a protesting Michael. 'We could do without the short people in there, if you can manage it.'

'We'll go for a walk,' Laura said. 'The rain's eased a bit. I was just telling Fiona about Dad.'

'He won't admit to anything, of course,' Alan confirmed, 'But your mum said she's seen him stopping in the middle of something and rubbing his shoulder.'

Fiona chewed her lip. 'It doesn't sound like Dad to stop in the middle of anything. I'm due for a long weekend soon. I'll make sure I get down to see them.'

'We're thinking of moving back ourselves,' Alan told her carefully. 'I've done all the research I need for my Ph.D. I only need to write it up and I could do that anywhere. Laura's dead keen to head south, of course.'

'The rebuilding's nearly finished on the shearer's cottage Mum and Dad are going to live in,' Laura added. 'They might be happy for us to take over the homestead now.'

Fiona had been listening quietly. She suddenly felt very subdued. 'What will I do with you guys gone?' she asked forlornly. Looking up, she found that Jonathan had joined them in time to hear the end of the conversation. Deliberately she pulled herself together. 'I mean, where would I find another crack decorating team at such short notice?'

Sometimes they could go for a couple of weeks without pre-term deliveries to contend with. The following week seemed to be entirely centred on such cases, with three deliveries at gestations of less than thirty weeks to Fiona's team. Jonathan made sure he was available at all stages and Doreen Roberts was, of course, also prominent.

Her frequent presence and the time spent in consultation with Jonathan Fletcher fuelled the rumours that they were an item. The staff, as always, enjoyed a background rumble of gossip, but when one of the midwives tried to engage Fiona in speculation she was disappointed.

'The bet is whether Dr Roberts will join the exodus to Wales, or will Mr Fletcher be tempted enough to stay here and go for Jack Owens' position?'

'It's really none of my business,' Fiona snapped. Her uncharacteristic tone and look left no doubt that it was also none of the midwife's business. Gossip within her earshot dropped off noticeably from that point.

Janet Redbury's progress continued to be satisfactory. Jonathan was delighted with the latest in the serial ultrasounds which showed an excellent rate of growth for the baby. Janet was being watched carefully now. No one knew how long their intervention would hold but each day was a bonus. Jonathan showed the results to Fiona.

'I think a lot of it has to do with how content she is to rest. Have you seen that amazing scrapbook she's working on?'

Fiona nodded.

'She's got the Redbury coat of arms now, from some relative in England, and the family tree goes back five generations. Whose idea was it, anyway?'

Fiona was silent, but Jonathan smiled wryly. 'I might have known.' He slotted Janet's ultrasound results carefully into her notes. 'It was a great idea,' he commented quietly. 'I hope you do it for your own children some day.'

Fiona had to turn away. The comment cut too deeply and she needed to hide the pain.

'Perhaps I will,' she replied tonelessly. Laura's voice echoed in her ears as she spoke. The suggestion her sister had made that she might be pregnant had been easy enough to dismiss at the time but had returned to haunt Fiona all week. At least Jonathan couldn't know the full effect of his comment.

The third pre-term case of the week was an elective Caesarean after premature rupture of the membranes at twenty-six weeks. They had prevented labour for several days in order to give steroids to aid the baby's lung development, but signs of foetal distress developed and it was decided that pre-term delivery by Caesarean was the safest option. Fiona had to admire the skill she observed as Doreen evaluated and resuscitated the tiny infant in Theatre.

Fiona tried to concentrate on assisting Jonathan as he continued with the surgery—removing the placenta and closing the uterus—but all the staff watched Doreen, waiting tensely.

The baby failed to respond to bag and mask ventilation so Doreen immediately went to endotracheal intubation. Leads were attached to check cardiac activity and an IV line was placed for drug administration as she worked with the baby under the heat of a radiant warmer. As soon as Doreen was satisfied that the baby was stable enough to transfer to the intensive care unit they put him into the double-walled incubator. Doreen nodded at Jonathan as her team left the theatre.

'We're doing fine so far,' she reported. 'Five minute Apgar score of four.'

Jonathan grunted. 'That's not too bad.'

Fiona removed the clamp as Jonathan finished his suture. She didn't think the score was great but said nothing. Jonathan sensed her disagreement.

'There's a sixty per cent mortality for pre-term babies with a five minute Apgar of zero to three,' he commented. 'That drops to fifteen per cent when it hits four. The odds are already considerably improved.'

Fiona watched Jonathan closing the abdominal wound. So many things in life depended on the odds, she mused. The newspapers and magazines were full of stories of happenings in spite of impossible odds. What about what Laura had said? Fiona was angry at the frequency with which her thoughts revolved around the suggestion. She resolved to sit down with a calendar that weekend to see if she could defuse the issue.

But her calculations with the calendar only served to increase the amazing speculation. Fiona was nearly ten days overdue, and the night of the wallpaper-stripping had been exactly mid-cycle.

'But it's not possible,' she muttered to herself over and over again. There had to be another explanation. Emotional stress could well be to blame. Fiona tried not to think of the ramifications if she was wrong. Being pregnant was not something she had planned or remotely wanted at this stage of her career.

'Don't cross bridges,' she warned herself. If she took an early-morning urine sample with her tomorrow, she would be able to drop into a chemist on the way home and have a test done. Or take a test home to administer in private. There would be time enough to worry, if necessary, once she knew for sure.

The sample was left shut in the glovebox of her car on Monday morning, but it might as well have been clutched in her hand for the influence it had on Fiona's thoughts. She almost walked straight past the large bunch of yellow roses in the ward office, but Jonathan made a point of directing her attention to it.

One glance at Martin's face before he made a hasty exit stopped Fiona misinterpreting the situation this time. Far from the correct message filtering through, it had clearly been modified to save embarrassment. Fiona sighed inwardly. She would have to see Tony today before this went any further. Louise breezed into the office and saw the bouquet.

'Not more roses!' she exclaimed.

'It would appear so.' Fiona was aware of raised eyebrows from Jonathan.

'Just as welcome as the last lot, I take it?' Louise was astute, but her tone in no way implied that she knew how Fiona felt. The eyes of the two women met and Fiona grinned at the proffered understanding.

'You're not wrong there, Louise.'

Jonathan left the office before Fiona crumpled the card, stuffing it into her pocket. Before her resolve could weaken she tried to beep Tony, but he was busy and Fiona herself was soon also distracted by work.

By chance she saw him as she headed towards the cafeteria at lunchtime. She signalled to him and they dropped to one side of the corridor out of the flow of human traffic.

'Thanks for the flowers, Tony. But please don't send me any more.'

'You don't like flowers?'

'That's not what I mean.' Fiona's face reflected her discomfort.

'I know. I get the message,' Tony said equably. 'No hard feelings?'

'No. I'm sorry, Tony.'

'I'm sorry too.'

The smile they exchanged was one of understanding, and Fiona felt relieved. Turning to leave, Fiona found herself being watched by Jonathan. He was standing a little further down the corridor in conversation with Philip Reece and Doreen Roberts. He gave a brief nod to Fiona and a long glance at Tony, then turned back to his companions. Fiona gave up on the idea of lunch and hurried back towards the ward. Her appetite seemed to desert her very easily these days.

Fiona chose the test offered at the chemist shop, rather than taking a test kit home. Somehow the results would seem more convincing if found by someone else. She had a nervous wait of ten minutes in the shop while the test was being done and spent the time examining the range of toothbrushes available. The girl came up to her side to speak discreetly.

'It's positive,' she said quietly.

Fiona kept staring at the toothbrushes in silence. The girl became embarrassed.

'I hope it's the result you wanted,' she said awkwardly, beginning to back away.

'Thanks.' Fiona was glad she had already paid for the test. Dazed, she walked from the shop back to her car, where she simply sat for twenty minutes, before starting the engine. It was only the thought of Belle needing to be let out that prompted her into movement. She couldn't believe it. And yet, now that she knew, it was perfectly believable. The subtle changes in her body and mood in the last couple of weeks all made perfect sense now.

The news seemed to be the final straw in the emotional upheaval of Fiona's life at present. Babies needed to be welcomed, ideally into a loving and stable environment. She certainly wasn't in the position to offer that. She was not ready to be a mother, despite the joy she gained from her nieces and nephews. And what of the father? It was the oldest trick in the book. The marriage trap.

It finally hit Fiona as she walked Belle home from the park. She had to laugh over the irony of it all. Here she had been agonising over a choice she hadn't needed to make. She would not have to live with a compromise for the rest of her life. This was Jonathan's baby. Her love for him naturally extended to their child. Of course she wanted it. She wanted 'the works', didn't she?

Jonathan wanted the same thing. He wanted it desperately but had given up hope of attaining it. And now Fiona could give it to him. They could both have it all. Practical and career considerations were forgotten as Fiona's excitement grew. She could just imagine the shock and then the joy lighting Jonathan's features when she broke the news. She could visualise them sitting wrapped in each other's arms—talking the night away as they cleared past grievances and made plans for their future.

It had a feeling of inevitability about it—something that was meant to happen. It made the tension and struggle to hide their feelings over the past weeks nothing more than a bad joke. Fiona couldn't wait to tell him. She raced home to the cottage and fed Belle, then hurriedly reheated the lentil casserole left over from last night. She would have to stop her habit of skipping meals.

While she ate, Fiona admired the finished living room. When the floorboards had been scrubbed and oiled they'd needed no further treatment, and Alan had come last night to help her move the furniture back into the room.

'Just as well,' Fiona told Belle. 'In my condition.'

The bright rag rug on the floor had been a finishing touch—a gift from Laura—and Fiona was thrilled at the fresh, cottagey feel to the room. She couldn't wait to start on the bedroom. In fact, the future looked so positive that Fiona felt she could tackle the entire house right now.

Belle came for a ride in the car to the hospital. Fiona drove past the main buildings to the staff hostel on the outskirts of the grounds. She checked the board near the front door to see what Jonathan's room number was, then ran happily up the stairs to knock on his door. She held her breath as she waited. Suppose he was out?

But he wasn't. His surprise quickly turned to curiosity as he caught something of Fiona's mood.

'What's up?' he asked. 'You're radiating happiness.'

Fiona knew she should wait until he invited her in—should break the news slowly so she could savour the moment—but her excitement bubbled over even as she still stood in the corridor.

'I just found out,' she said breathlessly. 'I'm pregnant!'

Fiona's smile was so broad it was almost painful. She eagerly watched Jonathan's face for his reaction. But the beloved features before her might have been carved of stone. After long, long moments of frightening immobility his lips moved slowly.

'Congratulations.'

Fiona's smile was rapidly subsiding. 'Aren't you pleased?'

'Of course.'

But he wasn't. If anything, he looked devastated. Fiona began to feel very confused. This was going very wrong and she couldn't even begin to understand why.

'I hope it's what you want,' Jonathan said with chilling courtesy.

'Isn't it what you want?' Fiona felt close to tears.

Jonathan gave a wry smile. 'Yes, I suppose it is. I want you to have the things I can't give you, Fiona. A baby is certainly at the top of that list.'

A glimmer of comprehension struck Fiona. She felt icy prickles of apprehension through her body.

'I take it that's what the flowers were all about—and your earnest conversation in the corridor at lunch-time.' Jonathan grinned lopsidedly. 'I must say you haven't wasted any time.'

'You're not suggesting—' Fiona was aware of an enormous anger welling within her. Anger at this betrayal mingled with all the past disappointments and turmoil. 'You bastard,' she breathed.

'You told me not to compare you with Clare, Fiona. And yet you come here, knowing how I feel about you, and tell me you're going to have another man's child.' Jonathan drew in a ragged breath. 'I don't think I deserve this. Why are you telling me?'

'Because it's *your* baby,' Fiona hissed. She was shaking with suppressed rage.

'You really expect me to believe that?' Jonathan gave a bitter laugh. 'What kind of fool do you take me for?'

'A bigger one than you'll ever realise.' Fiona straightened her back and looked long and hard at the man standing before her. 'I'll never forgive you for this, Jonathan Fletcher,' she said carefully. 'Never.'

And with that, Fiona Donaldson turned on her heel and strode away without a backward glance.

CHAPTER EIGHT

WHY, in God's name, had he ever agreed to make this journey?

Jonathan Fletcher had considered himself ready to cope with a partial return to his past. His life was on track now, and as satisfying as he could hope to make it.

There had never been any intention of involving himself again with any people from the past. The attraction had been the idea of revisiting old haunts, perhaps to exorcise past ghosts or at least view them from the perspective of being in control.

Once again life appeared to have given him a raw deal. Far from being in control, Jonathan felt as helpless and angry as he had as a child. Desperate then for someone to love—a person and place he could trust—he had tried repcatedly, only to find that things fell apart. It was a pattern he thought he had broken. After Clare he had vowed never to even approach a position where it could happen again.

This time seemed crueller than any in the past. In the space of the last month Jonathan had come to realise just how strong was his love for Fiona. The realisation had been unexpected. Overwhelming, really.

He'd known he loved her, but as a friend—or perhaps a sister. Well, there had been that kiss the night before he'd left all those years ago, but hadn't that just been part of the excitement of leaving? Funny how frequently it had popped into his memory over the years, though, with an indefinable feeling that had occasionally been disturbing.

The awakening of their sexual relationship now, combined with their past bond, made it so painfully obvious that this was what he had searched for throughout his life. Something perfect. He had been prepared to sacrifice it for her happiness—to give her the opportunity to find the sort of fulfilment in life that he would never have.

The sacrifice had been thrown back at him. She could not have known how she was repeating history with the words, 'I just found out—I'm pregnant'. It might as well have been Clare standing before him. The pain was immeasurably worse, however.

His relationship with Clare had never had even an inkling of the depth of feeling Jonathan had for Fiona. He had believed she might feel the same way about him. The thought that anyone could possibly feel like that about him had been a memory he intended to treasure for the rest of his life. That—and the intense memory of their lovemaking.

Yet through the pain came an insistent nagging thought that Fiona really believed she was telling the truth. Either that or his complete faith in her honesty had been misplaced. He felt betrayed and confused. Hurt and angry that the blow should come from a direction he had least expected.

Work was unbearable. Fiona openly avoided him. When he walked into a room she walked out. She ignored him in passing, and when forced to communicate she used his formal title with a subtle emphasis on the 'Mr'. The tension was obvious to everyone, and poor Martin Cox was caught in the middle, trying to provide a buffer while comforting his junior colleague and friend. He had no real idea what was going on, as far as Jonathan knew, but it was obvious to everyone that Fiona was miserable.

Her duties were performed as skilfully and meticulously as ever, but her hazel eyes looked too large in the pale face, her vibrant demeanour was dulled, her voice was quiet and personal exchanges nonexistent.

After only two days of this, Jonathan could no longer stand it. He made his way towards the office of the chairman of the department. There had to be a way he could return home early, without causing too much inconvenience. After all, they would have to find a locum in the wake of Jack Owens' proposed resignation.

His beeper went before he reached the office, and Jonathan changed direction after the phone call, going towards the obstetric ward. He saw Fiona writing busily in some case notes and closed the door of the office behind them. Fiona acknowledged his presence with a nod but did not look at him.

'Mrs Julie Williamson, aged twenty-five years, primigravida at thirty weeks gestation,' Fiona recited carefully, as though reading a mental list. 'Uneventful pregnancy up till now. Last check with her GP was a week ago and showed nothing untoward, apart from a trace of protein in her urine. She was due to have a follow-up appointment tomorrow. She collapsed and had a convulsion at home this morning and was brought straight in by ambulance. She was given diazepam in A and E. We've started magnesium sulphate to prevent further convulsions and an infusion of labetalol to reduce her blood pressure, which is presently one eighty over one twenty-five.'

Jonathan whistled in dismay. There was no response from Fiona.

'Platelet count is well down at ninety-three, there's marked proteinuria but there's no evidence of foetal distress at this point.'

'Good.' Jonathan shook his head. 'It's pretty rare to see a case of eclampsia like this, but it can come on with astonishing speed. You've done all the right things so far. Well done.'

'Martin admitted her,' Fiona said flatly. 'I'm just monitoring the situation. There's a difficult delivery on downstairs.'

Jonathan sighed. So he wasn't even to offer professional encouragement or praise. He wished Martin was still here.

'We'll have to stabilise her first, of course,' he said briskly, 'but in view of the convulsions we can't justify delaying delivery any longer than that. Watch the labetalol infusion. You should get control at a rate of between twenty-four and forty-eight millilitres per hour.

'I'll contact Paediatrics as soon as I've seen Mrs Williamson, and you can get in touch with Anaesthetics. It'll have to be a Caesar at this stage, to give us a controlled delivery for both the mother and baby. There's a greater risk of complications with a general so we'll have to go for an epidural. Fill them in carefully, please. We're going to have to watch fluid management as well.'

Jonathan paused. Even with his mind fixed on this emergency, he could not fail to notice how wretched Fiona looked. The inner voice nagged at him again.

What if—it was a big if—but what if there was a remote possibility that Fiona was right?

When he had a free moment late that afternoon Jonathan sought out Philip Reece. He made sure their conversation couldn't be overheard before he spoke.

'It's a rather delicate matter,' he began awkwardly, 'and one that I would like to remain confidential.'

'Of course.' Philip looked puzzled, but intrigued.

'You took over running the IVF programme when I opted out, didn't you?'

'That's correct. Did you want to change your mind about getting involved?'

'No, sorry.' Jonathan shook his head regretfully. 'What I'd like is to have a check-up done—discreetly, if possible.' Jonathan fidgeted with his stethoscope and then cleared his throat. 'A semen analysis.'

'For yourself?'

Jonathan hesitated and then nodded briefly. He gave Philip a quick rundown of his history and previous findings. 'I'd just like to know if the situation has changed at all.' He laughed lightly. 'It would be less embarrassing to do it on this side of the world than on my home patch.'

'Of course. I don't see why we can't put a sample through anonymously, in any case. I'll let you know what's required.'

This time Jonathan's laugh was genuine. 'I think I have a fair idea.'

It took over twelve hours to stabilise Julie Williamson's blood pressure enough for Jonathan to consider it safe to proceed with the Caesarean. The case had attracted a lot of attention, and senior paediatric and anaesthetic staff were on hand because of the risk of complications. In consequence, the theatre was crowded, and Fiona shook her head at Martin as she peered through the scrub-room doors.

'It's a real circus in there. I'm only going to be in the way. I don't suppose anyone will miss me if I sneak off.'

'I will.' Martin smiled at Fiona. He hated seeing her like this, especially now that he was so happy. 'Shall we sneak off together?'

He was rewarded with a brief smile.

'I wish I could help, Fiona. It's not Tony, making a nuisance of himself, is it?'

'No, not at all. Don't worry, Martin. I'll be just fine. Besides, you're already helping. Covering for me on Friday so I can take a break is exactly what I need.' Her smile brightened. 'You'll see, I'll be a new woman by the time I get back on Monday.'

'Not too new, I hope,' Martin grinned. 'The old one was just fine by me.'

It was late on Thursday afternoon by the time Jonathan caught Philip Reece privately. They spent several minutes discussing the successful outcome of Julie Williamson's case and how well the tiny baby was doing, then the older consultant closed the door to his office before handing Jonathan a manila envelope containing a printout. Jonathan scanned the results in silence.

'Pretty much the same as last time,' he said finally.

'Had you expected a change?'

'Not really. Something just prompted me to think about it again.' He looked at the damning sheet of paper for a long moment and then glanced at Philip.

'In your opinion, what would the odds be of me fathering a child in natural circumstances?'

Philip looked very thoughtful. 'I wouldn't rush off to buy any teddy bears,' he said slowly.

'No. I thought not.'

'But neither would I rely on it for a defence in a paternity suit,' smiled Philip. 'Unlikely things have a habit of occurring far more often than the law of averages allows for.'

'Yes. That thought has also occurred to me.'

Jonathan felt strangely calm after his interview with Philip. Somehow things seemed to have fallen into place. He went straight to an outpatient clinic where he found his senior registrar between patients.

'Do you know what's going on between Fiona Donaldson and Tony Lloyd?' he asked without preamble.

Martin looked taken aback. 'Absolutely nothing. I fixed them up for an evening with us at the casino. He pestered Fiona by sending her flowers on a couple of occasions, but as far as I'm aware she cleared up any misunderstanding. Is there a problem?'

'Yes,' Jonathan muttered, more to himself, then he saw Martin's expression. 'Not with Tony, though. Where's Fiona?'

'I sent her home early. She wasn't looking so great.'

Jonathan nodded. 'Can you manage the rest of the clinic?'

'Sure. We're nearly done.'

'Great. Thanks Martin. I'll catch you tomorrow.'

Jonathan walked from the hospital to Fiona's cottage to try and give himself time. Perhaps something could be done to patch up their relationship. He couldn't head back to the other side of the world without at least trying to clear some of the ill-feeling—on both sides. Jonathan still felt confused. And angry. Added to that now was a terrible misgiving that maybe he had misjudged Fiona.

He had been the first, he knew that. Did he really believe she could have turned and jumped into bed with someone else simply because he'd said they had no future? If nothing else, he intended to find out the truth. Surely he deserved that much, even if he was responsible for the mess they were in.

But the cottage seemed empty, and there was no bark from Belle to indicate that her owner might be due home soon. Fiona was probably round at Laura and Alan's, Jonathan decided. He couldn't talk to her there.

He rang every hour that evening. The phone was answered at 9 p.m., but as soon as Fiona heard his voice she hung up. The calls at 10 and 11 p.m. went unanswered. At midnight the engaged signal indicated that the phone had been taken off the hook.

Jonathan didn't even bother trying to go to bed that night. Sleep was as elusive as the solution to the mess he had created. The more he brooded over it the more he doubted his own assessment of the situation. Perhaps Fiona wasn't pregnant. It was almost too soon to know for sure. Emotional stress was well known to affect cycles and, God knew, she had had plenty of that recently.

Assuming that she was, indeed, pregnant, what if the baby *was* his and he had finally crushed their relationship totally with his reaction? The thought was not one he wanted to live with. Even if the baby wasn't his, couldn't they have built something around that? It might have been the perfect compromise. By 7 a.m. he was back at the hospital, hoping somehow that he might catch Fiona and persuade her to listen, even for just a minute or two.

He checked the wards, offices and labour suite unsuccessfully. He waited until 8.30 and then repeated the circuit. He didn't try beeping her, convinced that only a personal approach would have the remotest chance of success. He was beeped himself, before completing the next search, and for the rest of the morning he found himself forced to concentrate on professional matters.

Janet Redbury was causing some concern. The scrapbook was forgotten for the moment and she seemed restless. She was getting an occasional contraction and complained of backache. Jonathan intensified the monitoring and ordered a repeat course of steroids.

'Just to be on the safe side,' he told Janet.

'Where's Fiona?' Janet queried. 'I'd like to see her.'

'I wish I knew,' Jonathan replied. 'I'd like to see her myself.'

At lunchtime he wandered around again, puzzled at Fiona's noticeable absence. Certainly she had been avoiding him at work, but it had never before been this well engineered. He had a quiet afternoon planned, with nothing but paperwork and a lecture to prepare. Surely he could corner her somewhere. Finally he beeped her. There was no response. He beeped Martin.

'I need to speak to Fiona,' he said, more curtly than he had intended. 'Where the hell is she?'

'Sorry, didn't I tell you? She's taken a day's leave. She won't be in till Monday. Can I help?'

'I doubt it.' Jonathan rang off, chiding himself for his rudeness. Another apology he would have to make.

The attempt to get a response from phoning the cottage proved futile. Jonathan paced his office. There had to be something he could do to resolve this—some way out of this unbearable turmoil. Suddenly he knew exactly what he needed to do. It was so simple—why hadn't it occurred to him earlier?

He thumbed through the telephone directory, then picked up the phone and gained an outside line. He rang through to the reservations desk at the Christchurch international airport.

'I need to make some urgent travel arrangements,' he said decisively. 'For this afternoon, if possible.'

Jonathan Fletcher was going home.

CHAPTER NINE

FIONA DONALDSON was also going home.

It was a long drive and she took her time, with frequent rest stops—both for Belle's sake and to wake herself up. She had had an almost sleepless night and had spent most of it staring at the telephone beside her bed, the receiver off its hook. What had he been so desperate to tell her that had prompted those earlier incessant calls? Perhaps he had decided she was telling the truth, after all, and he had decided to claim fatherhood.

Well, it was too late for that. Much too late. It had been a final betrayal and Fiona Donaldson was going to make sure it remained final.

Her route took her into the central part of South Island, past the bright blue of Lake Tekapo, where she stopped for a leisurely break in the early afternoon. She was much later than she had intended to be, having finally fallen asleep just before dawn. In her exhausted state she had slept right through her alarm, not waking until mid-morning.

At this rate, it would be well after dark by the time she reached the farm, but she was in no hurry. Her parents wouldn't be anxious about a late arrival because Fiona hadn't told them she was coming.

Fiona told herself it was because she wanted the visit to be a surprise, but she knew she was denying the real reason. She feared her mother would detect an undercurrent in their conversation. Fiona had no desire to be greeted by probing enquiries, no matter how tactful or lovingly meant. For now, it was enough to be headed in the direction of home. The solitude and calm of the trip was giving her time to ponder how her parents would react to her news.

That was if she decided to tell them at this point. Fiona was anxious to find out just how well her father was before she burdened them with her worries. Her own problems weren't going to go away in a hurry and she could afford to wait if need be. She needed their supportive love more than anything, and she knew that was waiting for her whether or not she revealed her situation.

When she'd cleared the Lindis Pass on her way south to Queenstown, Fiona felt she was on home territory. She negotiated the notorious Kawara Gorge with pleasure and found her speed inching up as she neared Frankton. Bypassing the route into the township of Queenstown, Fiona skirted the side of Lake Wakatipu, now in gloomy darkness under the shadow of the Remarkables.

The final glimmer of daylight had faded as Fiona closed the last of the farm gates behind her and drove down the long tree-lined driveway. The windows of the homestead glowed welcomingly and Fiona felt bathed with relief. This had definitely been the right place to come.

Fiona opened the front door, without knocking, and surveyed the wide hallway with pleasure. The rich red of the carpet runner was enhanced by the subdued lighting and stretched invitingly along the considerable length of the hallway before flowing up the curved staircase at the end. The house was very quiet, and the closed doors, with no light showing beneath, indicated that the living areas at the front of the house were unoccupied. That was not unexpected.

Fiona knew that, when on their own, her parents used very little of the large house. Apart from their bedroom and bathroom upstairs, they tended to live in the huge farmhouse kitchen. Still heated by the ancient coal range, installed when the house was built more than a hundred years ago, it had always been the heart of the house. The inviting warmth of the room was independent of the seasons or use of the range. One end of the room accommodated several chairs and couches, bookshelves and a television. Fiona knew that was where her parents would be now.

Pausing in the hallway, Fiona wished she had stopped somewhere along the way and rung to let them know she was coming. She wanted to surprise them, not frighten them. She looked down at Belle, sitting by her feet, her tail waving slowly as she watched Fiona's face.

'Come on, girl. Let's find everyone.' Fiona set off towards the door beneath the stairwell. It was partly ajar and she called out cheerfully as they neared it.

'Hi! It's only me.'

Belle pushed through the door ahead of her, and Fiona grinned as she heard the startled exclamations. She walked happily into the kitchen—then stopped, as though she had walked into a wall. Her parents were not alone. Sitting with them was Jonathan Fletcher.

'What the hell are you doing here?'

Belle had made a delighted beeline for Jonathan, but now threw herself down at the tone of Fiona's voice. Her mother rose to her feet just as quickly.

'Darling! What a wonderful surprise. Why didn't you tell us you were coming?'

'I wouldn't have come—' Fiona was still staring at Jonathan in horror '—if I had known you already had a visitor.'

'Steady on, Fiona.' Matthew Donaldson's deep voice was gruff.

Ruth Donaldson reached her daughter and gave her a warm hug. Fiona's lips felt stiff as she kissed her mother.

'Have you eaten?'

'I'm not very hungry.' Fiona tried to ignore the beseeching look in her mother's eyes but couldn't. She gave her another, more heartfelt kiss. 'It's good to see you, Mum.'

Jonathan was collecting empty cups and saucers from the coffee-table. Fiona ignored him and walked towards her father. She bent and kissed his weather-beaten cheek.

'How are you, Dad?'

'Nothing wrong with me.' Matthew Donaldson nodded at Jonathan. 'Thanks, lad. You'll find something a bit stronger than that in the cupboard beside the fridge. I think we could all use a drop right now.'

'Not for me, thanks.' Fiona was aware of sudden tension and looked sharply at her mother, then she whirled to face the retreating figure of Jonathan.

'Just what have you been telling my parents?' she demanded. He turned back and set down his tray, but she hadn't needed to ask. One look at their faces told Fiona that her parents already knew. Not only had the sanctuary of her home been invaded, even her choice of temporary privacy was gone. Fiona was furious.

'How could you?' she shouted. 'Haven't you already done enough?'

'Fiona!' There was a warning in her father's voice that brought back more than a few childhood memories. 'Jonathan will always be a welcome guest in this house. He's a part of this family, as far as I'm concerned.'

'How can you say that?' Fiona rounded on her father. 'After the way he just deserted us all. You watched Mum worry about him on and off for years. I never heard you defending him then.'

'Please, darling. Give him a chance.' Ruth's tone was conciliatory. 'At least give him a chance to explain.'

'Oh, I did that,' Fiona replied bitterly. 'And look where it got me.'

'I'm sorry.' Jonathan spoke for the first time since Fiona had entered the room. 'Perhaps I shouldn't have come.'

'Of course you should,' Ruth said firmly. 'As you said yourself, it's the only real home you've ever had. It's where you needed to come.'

'Find that whisky, lad,' Matthew said. He was clearly distressed by the scene he found himself in and felt unable to handle it. He rose a little stiffly from his chair. 'On second thoughts, I'll find it myself.'

Fiona glared angrily at Jonathan. She saw no anger reflected in his eyes, only sadness—which undermined the emotional base she had instinctively chosen. She sighed heavily.

'I'll go upstairs,' she said evenly. 'It's too late to travel tonight. I'll head back to Christchurch in the morning.'

'Oh, no!' Ruth shook her head. 'You can't do that.'

'There's no need,' Jonathan said quietly. 'I'll go.'

'Nonsense.' Fiona's father returned, carrying a decanter and glasses. 'You'll both stay and we'll get this lot sorted. Can't have this sort of a carry-on. It's not good for anybody.'

'You're not wrong there, Dad,' Fiona agreed. 'And I've had enough for now. If you'll excuse me, I'll see you in the morning.'

She felt no small measure of satisfaction in the way Belle instantly deserted Jonathan to follow her upstairs, but the feeling vanished as soon as she was alone in her room. What an intolerable mess she was in. Hoping to find refuge, and a break to come to terms with her situation, Fiona had instead found herself confronted by war.

On the one side she had herself—and Belle, of course. Fiona dropped a hand to the soft head resting on her knee. Her cause felt righteous enough—abandoned initially, given and then denied hope, and finally the ultimate betrayal. She'd had not only her honesty but her commitment to the person she had loved questioned.

Had loved. Was it really the past tense? Could she really deny that beneath the anger the feelings and commitment remained intact?

On the other side of the battle was Jonathan. Now he clearly had the weight of her own parents' support—and on her home ground. But was it only hers? she argued with herself. Hadn't she always considered that Jonathan was also a part of this family? That this was where he belonged?

Fiona was relieved at the interruption to her confused thoughts caused by the knock at her door. Her mother entered, carrying a tray laden with a steaming bowl of thick vegetable soup and a plate of home-made crusty rolls.

'No butter—I didn't forget.' Ruth smiled tentatively as she set down the tray. She laid a gentle hand on her daughter's head. 'I'm so glad you're home, darling.'

Ruth paused, and then sat on the bed beside Fiona. 'Jon rang us at lunchtime to ask if he could come. We had got over the surprise by the time he arrived this afternoon, and we've done nothing but talk ever since.' Ruth sighed lightly. 'He's been through a lot, and right now I think he's suffering more than he ever has before.'

'He's not the only one,' Fiona said quickly.

'I know. We want to help, darling, but I think the only way through is for you both to talk to each other. Really talk.'

'We've said too much already.' Fiona's tone was hopeless.

'Or perhaps not enough.' Ruth Donaldson rose to her feet and then bent to kiss Fiona. 'Think about it—and sleep well.'

Surprisingly, Fiona did sleep well. She woke late and, finding Belle eager for release, she dressed hurriedly in jodhpurs and a warm jersey. In the kitchen she found her father and Jonathan finishing their second breakfast. They had been up since 6 a.m., covering many miles on the farm bikes checking the sheep. Lambing season was much later in the high country, to allow for more favourable conditions. It wouldn't hit its peak for another couple of weeks, but some early arrivals were already keeping them busy. Fiona looked at the box beside the coal range. Empty for the moment, it would house its annual quota of orphans before the season finished. Jonathan had been watching her.

'Remember Ivan?' he asked quietly.

Fiona was silent. Of course she remembered. How could she ever forget the night when she had discovered that she loved the sad stranger who had joined their family?

'How is he?' Jonathan tried to fill the awkward silence.

Now Fiona did look at Jonathan. 'He died,' she said coldly, 'a long time ago.'

During the new silence Fiona cut herself a thick slice of bread from the loaf on the table and spread it with honey. She did not sit down.

'I think I'll go for a ride,' she informed her mother. 'I could do with some fresh air.'

'Oh... Do you think that's a good idea, darling?'

Fiona looked at the concerned faces around her and instinctively her hand went to her belly.

'All right,' she said in exasperation. 'I'll go for a walk.'

It was a long walk and Fiona kept up a brisk pace. At first she walked quickly, because she was irritated that she was not on horseback as she would have preferred. Had she been on her own, she would probably not have thought twice about riding. The risk of a fall was so slight, and the exercise was one to which her body was well accustomed.

It was the obvious assumption of others that she was not prepared to challenge. It was not even so much the obstacle to her riding that was so irritating, but that her right to choose seemed to have been taken away from her. In this and other, more important areas of her life.

Fiona Donaldson was accustomed to choosing her own way through life, and also accustomed to being successful. She had chosen her hobbies and sports in dog trials and showjumping, and her achievements at an early age were now something of a local legend. She had also chosen and excelled in the subjects she'd wanted at school, then had chosen her career, graduating with a distinction which had also marked her houseman years.

She hadn't exactly chosen Jonathan initially—that had just happened. But this time around it had been a definite choice and one in which she had thought, briefly, that she could succeed. And now she was pregnant, and that wasn't of her choosing either. Fiona felt overtaken by recent events, swamped by them. She also felt she was failing in something of far greater importance than life had ever previously presented. Success in any direction seemed remote.

The irritation which had prompted the brisk pace of walking mellowed but Fiona kept up the pace. The stimulation of the exercise, particularly uphill as she was now heading, was beneficial to her mood. Perhaps if she could make it right up to the brow of the hill, without stopping, she might even see a glimmer of a solution.

Fiona hadn't noticed the significance of the path she had chosen. Neither had she noticed that she was being followed. When she finally stopped, well out of breath, and flopped down into the tussock she was very surprised to see Jonathan toiling up the hill in her wake. Surprised and annoyed. She wasn't ready to talk to him. She had a lot more talking to herself to do first. Jonathan was very out of breath by the time he reached the hilltop. He threw himself down flat on his back.

'How on earth do you keep yourself so fit?' he gasped.

'I've got youth on my side—have you forgotten?'

Jonathan sat up slowly. 'I haven't forgotten.' He was silent for several minutes. Fiona made no move to break the silence so they both sat quietly, looking at the view rather than each other.

'There's something else I haven't forgotten either,' Jonathan said softly.

Fiona could feel his gaze on her but didn't turn her head.

'Oh?' Her tone lacked any encouragement.

'The last time we sat on this particular hill. Do you remember?'

The memory flooded back. The sunset, the imminent departure—and the kiss. The kiss that had stayed with her for so many years. Fiona cursed herself for choosing this route for her walk and then smiled grimly to herself. Perhaps that hadn't really been a choice either.

'Yes, I remember,' she said woodenly. And that's an understatement if ever I heard one, she added silently. If only he knew.

'It haunted me for a long time,' Jonathan told her. 'I had the feeling I had made a mistake but I couldn't put my finger on what it was.'

Fiona was silent. She waited for what she thought was coming. An apology, perhaps even a proposal—a proposal she had no intention of accepting or encouraging. In fact, she didn't want to hear it. She moved, in preparation to get to her feet, but Jonathan's voice stalled her.

'When you get hurt, really hurt, it becomes difficult to trust someone.' His tone was almost detached, as though speaking simply in general terms. 'When it happens more than once it becomes more difficult.' Fiona felt his gaze turned on her again.

'It can become hard to trust even oneself. Perhaps the worst is to be hurt by the person you truly love, one in whom you had absolute trust. That pain can be unbearable and you feel compelled to run and hide, at the very least, on an emotional level.'

Fiona gave an almost imperceptible nod but couldn't look at Jonathan. Was he talking about Clare hurting him, Jonathan hurting herself or possibly the way she, Fiona, was now treating him?

'It's easy to run, Pen,' Jonathan said gently. 'I know. I also know it isn't the answer.'

Fiona was still sitting on the tussock. It was Jonathan who rose to his feet. He stood looking down at the homestead, and then his gaze rose to the lake and the mountains.

'This is still the most beautiful place on earth,' he said wistfully. He took a few steps in a homeward direction and then turned.

'You told me recently that I was a bigger fool than I would ever realise. You were wrong there, Pen.'

Fiona finally looked up. She met his eyes steadily but was aware of the faint lopsided smile.

'I realise it only too well.'

Fiona watched the long strides that carried Jonathan swiftly down the hill. She sat for a long time, mulling over the one-sided conversation. It hadn't exactly been an apology. It hadn't exactly been an explanation. But it had been something. Fiona felt calmer. She could sense the promise of being able to think and then to talk about the issues involved. Perhaps resolution was even possible. By the time Fiona rose and stretched, ready for the hike back home, she felt confident. Not exactly optimistic, but confident that whatever came of it all she could still succeed. There were still some choices she could make.

Arriving back at the homestead just as lunch was being served, Fiona was glad the small amount of bustle precluded any private conversation. She made an effort to be cheerful but the talk was sporadic and kept up mainly due to the efforts of Ruth. Fiona noticed Jonathan giving her father frequent glances during the course of the meal and she wondered why.

Matthew Donaldson hadn't eaten much and was certainly looking uncomfortable. Fiona sighed, knowing that she had largely created a situation he was finding distressing. She also noticed him rubbing his shoulder, and the older man seemed to be finding the kitchen overly warm. Beads of perspiration shone on his face.

Ruth Donaldson was watching her husband with concern as well. 'I'm sorry. I shouldn't have stoked up the range, but I thought it was getting cool.'

'Are you all right, Matt?' Jonathan's voice had an edge that filled Fiona with alarm.

'Of course I'm all right.' Matthew Donaldson rose to his feet slowly. 'I just need some fresh air.'

Silently Jonathan left the table and followed him outside. Fiona and her mother exchanged glances, then they, too, rose and went to the back door. Fiona watched as her father's steps slowed and stopped, and then Jonathan took his arm supportively.

She expected her father to shrug off the assistance, but to her horror she saw him slump into the younger man's arms as he collapsed. Jonathan had laid Matthew carefully on the ground by the time Fiona reached them. She threw herself into a crouch beside her father's head.

'He's not breathing.' Fiona stared in panic at Jonathan. Fear overwhelmed her and suddenly she had no idea what she should do. 'Help him, Jon.'

Jonathan took his fingers from Matthew Donaldson's neck. He raised both hands to form a fist and landed a massive thump on the lower part of Matthew's chest. Then he changed his hand grip and began to compress the chest rhythmically.

'Breathe for him, Pen. On the count of five.'

Fiona tilted her father's head back, checked his airway was clear then pinched his nose and sealed his lips with her own. She heard Jonathan count five, then filled her father's lungs with the breath from her own. She listened as Jonathan began counting his compressions again. She repeated the breaths several times, thankful that her task was being directed for her.

'OK, stop for a minute.' Jonathan knelt over Matthew, his fingers again feeling for a pulse.

'He's breathing again,' Fiona whispered.

'And his rhythm's reverted to normal.' Jonathan still sounded tense. 'Ruth, have you got an aspirin?'

'Yes, of course, but what on earth—?'

Jonathan cut off her puzzled protest. 'Get it, please. And grab some blankets. Pen, have you got an emergency kit in your car?'

'Yes.' Fiona was already on her feet. 'I'll get it.'

Matthew Donaldson was regaining consciousness rapidly.

'Don't move for the moment, Matt,' Jonathan ordered. 'We've got a wee way to go yet. How's the pain?'

Fiona and her mother arrived back at the same time, less than a minute later. Ruth handed over an aspirin tablet, which Jonathan pressed into Matthew's mouth.

'Chew that,' he said firmly. 'It'll work faster that way.'

'I can't believe that's going to help,' Ruth protested. 'He's having a heart attack, isn't he?'

'Looks that way,' Jonathan agreed. 'And an aspirin's one of the best things we can give him at this point. A heart attack is caused by a blood clot blocking an artery. Aspirin affects the platelets in the blood—makes it less sticky. It's one of the spanners we like to throw in the works of the clotting process.' He looked at Fiona. 'Have you got an IV cannula and some saline or haemaccel in your kit?'

Fiona nodded.

'Morphine?'

She was already sorting through the contents of her well-stocked bag.

'Let's give him 2.5mg of morphine and set up an IV line, then.' Jonathan sounded calm. His presence and control held back the shock Fiona was feeling. She found she was responding to him with a desperate eagerness, functioning without trying to analyse. Her trust in him was complete.

'I don't suppose you have a beta blocker, have you?'

'No, sorry.' Fiona bit her lip. 'I was thinking of road accidents when I made up the kit.'

'Let's get him in the car and to hospital. Unless there's a helicopter service available?'

Ruth shook her head. 'Not quickly, at any rate. And the ambulance would probably take even longer.'

'Right.' Jonathan made adjustments to the IV line and handed the plastic bag to Fiona. 'You can be the pole,' he told her with a quick smile. 'We'll get in the back of the station wagon with him. Are you all right to drive, Ruth?'

She nodded, impressing her daughter with her calm manner. Fiona felt ready to go to pieces and was sure she would have done so if it had not been for Jonathan. What good would her training have been then if she couldn't have used it to save her own father?

Ruth Donaldson drove swiftly but carefully. They arrived at the district hospital in Queenstown in less than thirty minutes. Jonathan was introduced to the retiring physician, Jim Holden, but took charge of the emergency himself.

The ECG showed definite changes due to a heart attack and Jonathan ordered an IV dose of a beta blocker, atenolol.

'We need to set up some thrombolysis,' he said to Dr Holden. 'Have you got streptokinase?'

Jim Holden shook his head.

'Can we transfer him? Where's the nearest coronary care unit?'

'Dunedin—but that's four hours by ambulance. I'll get hold of the airport to see what flights are scheduled for Christchurch.'

Jonathan glanced over to where Ruth sat, holding

her husband's hand, and then shook his head at Fiona. 'To be effective we need the streptokinase within four to six hours after the infarct. We've lost an hour already.'

Jim Holden turned from the phone. 'There's a flight just boarding for Christchurch now. They'll hold for twenty minutes if we can be ready.'

Jonathan nodded emphatically and waited until Jim replaced the receiver.

'We're going to need full rescusitation equipment for the flight. Defibrillator, endotracheal tube, ambu bag, oxygen...' Jonathan's list continued rapidly. Jim was already collecting some of the gear, and he handed Fiona the key to the drugs cabinet as Jonathan finished his list. 'Lignocaine, adrenaline, atropine. Oh, and some narcaine, just in case we need to reverse the effects of the narcotics.'

Jim was adding a blood-pressure cuff and stethoscope to the pile on the trolley. 'I thought you were an obstetrician,' he muttered. 'How come you sound so much like a cardiologist?'

Jonathan grinned. 'A good general knowledge is always useful, I've found.'

Two men in St John's Ambulance uniforms came into the room with a stretcher. Jonathan went back to Matthew.

'We're going to take you somewhere a bit more high-tech,' he explained. 'We're heading for the coronary care unit in Christchurch.'

Matthew nodded. He was looking frightened but Fiona saw in the eyes of both her parents the same trust she now realised she had in Jonathan Fletcher.

The transfer from the hospital to the airport and into the plane had a nightmare quality about it that Fiona knew she would never forget. At the centre of it all Jonathan remained calm and reassuring. As they boarded the plane Fiona suddenly grew agitated.

'Belle—we've just left her.'

Jonathan adjusted the oxygen mask on Matthew's face and turned to the ambulance officer.

'Can you contact the police to get them to secure the Donaldsons' farm?' He smiled at Fiona. 'There's a Border collie there that will need some special attention.'

'Get them to call our neighbours, the Taylors,' Ruth Donaldson added. 'Gwen will know what to do.'

The flight was only about an hour in duration but it seemed much longer to Fiona. As she watched the ECG monitor on the life pack she noticed the heart rate dropping into a bradycardia. Feeling her father's forehead, she found his skin clammy. He was sweating again.

'Jon!' Her tone was pleading.

'It's OK, Pen.' Jonathan was already filling a small syringe. He caught Fiona's eye. 'Trust me?'

Their eyes locked for a second as Fiona nodded. The message was deeper than even their emergency situation warranted, and they were both aware of it.

'This is atropine,' Jonathan explained quickly. 'It should counter the bradycardia, which is probably being accentuated by the beta blocker or the morphine.'

The rate at which Matthew Donaldson's heart was beating rose steadily after administration of the drug, but Fiona kept her eyes glued to the ECG screen. She was aware of Jonathan's ceaseless monitoring of his patient, checking his rhythm, blood pressure, colour, and listening to both his heart and lungs at regular intervals. She could hear her mother making soft, comforting conversation with her husband. Through it all Fiona was aware that her anger towards Jonathan had vanished.

She *did* trust him. More than anyone on earth. No matter what might be said in the heat of the moment, she could never doubt his loyalty and love for her. She thought it more than likely he now believed the same of her. She just hadn't given him the chance to express it.

The chance was further delayed on their arrival in Christchurch with Matthew's transfer to the coronary care unit. Jonathan handed over his patient at that point, but Matthew insisted on having him present as his treatment continued.

Fiona and her mother waited nervously in the relatives' area, and Ruth used the time to phone her neighbour, leaving a list of instructions concerning the farm.

Fiona used the other phone to call both Daniel and Laura. The family was gathering its resources and Fiona felt buoyed by the strength of their bond. Perhaps Jonathan was right, she thought fleetingly. Family *is* everything.

Laura arrived at the hospital in time to hear the news from Jonathan that the streptokinase had been given in time and the ECG changes were now reverting to normal. Ruth and Laura went in to see Matthew, leaving Fiona and Jonathan alone together. They were silent for a minute, but both were aware that the silence lacked the tension they had previously felt.

Jonathan reached out his hands and took hold of Fiona's.

'This isn't the right time to talk, Pen. For two reasons. One is that your Dad, your family and yourself are going to need all your strength and attention for the next few days.' He gave her hands a squeeze and then gently let them go. 'The other reason is that I've dug my own grave in a way. I've made you believe that I think there are things more important than just us. I don't expect you to believe that's changed, irrespective of the altered circumstances, and I don't want to insult you by making assumptions I have no right to make.'

Fiona opened her mouth to speak, but Jonathan touched her lips gently with his finger.

'Don't say anything. Please, Pen. Let everything settle for a few days at least—a few weeks, if you need to. I'm not going anywhere just yet. If and when I do go, it certainly won't be before you and I have said everything that needs to be said.'

Fiona nodded. 'Thank you,' she said softly. Standing on tiptoe, she gave Jonathan's cheek a brief kiss. 'Thank you for what you've just said, but even more for what you did today. Our family wouldn't still be together if it hadn't been for you.'

Later that night Fiona used her professional capacity to sneak an extra visit into the CCU. She sat quietly by her father's bed, holding his hand and watching the ECG monitor. Matthew Donaldson appeared to be sleeping, so Fiona was startled when he spoke to her.

'Bit of a hero, isn't he?'

Fiona nodded, smiling. There was no doubt he was referring to Jonathan.

'He's in love with you, you know.'

Fiona nodded again.

'And you love him, don't you, Fiona?' Matthew's voice grew slower. He was tiring.

'I always have, Dad.'

'Better marry the lad, then.' Matthew gave his daughter's hand an encouraging pat.

Fiona chuckled. 'There's just one problem there, Dad.'

The voice was now a sleepy mumble. 'What's that?'

'He hasn't asked me.'

CHAPTER TEN

THE next day or so passed in something of a blur.

The Donaldson clan gathered. Daniel arrived from Auckland on Saturday evening, and Fiona made up the couch at the cottage for him to sleep on. Ruth was staying with Laura and Alan, although much of her time was spent at the hospital. They took turns to visit Matthew so as not to tire him too much. When the family wasn't at the hospital, their time was spent caring for and entertaining the children and preparing and consuming meals. And talking.

The unity and common resolve of the family conferences, as the Donaldsons suggested and moulded plans for the future, impressed Fiona, and she was pleased that they automatically included Jonathan.

He was clearly the family hero, his advice and company eagerly sought. It was Jonathan who brought the good news on Sunday evening that Matthew's blood tests showed an early peak and drop of the enzymes associated with infarction. Combined with the results of other tests, the prognosis for a full recovery was excellent.

That meal turned into a real celebration and the conference that night was optimistic and productive.

It was decided that Matthew and Ruth would move into the small but comfortable farm cottage as soon as Matthew was released from hospital. Daniel was delegated to contact the local builders and decorators to ensure that the house would be ready. Laura and

Alan were going to take over management of the farm immediately. It was the ideal solution but it would require a lot of planning. Fiona found herself helping Laura and Ruth begin packing almost immediately. Alan, Daniel and Jonathan were also busy sorting out details of organisation. Apparently, these meetings were more successful when conducted at the nearby pub!

Work continued throughout it all. Fiona knew that Jonathan and Martin would make things as easy as possible for her, but she felt guilty at not pulling her weight. Having missed Theatre completely on Monday morning, she was determined to do her share of the antenatal clinic that afternoon. She was beeped and called to the ward even before her first patient was ushered in.

She found Janet Redbury distressed. Having settled again over the weekend, the monitors now showed that contraction frequency and strength had increased markedly. Fiona examined her quickly.

'I think Daisy's pretty keen to make an appearance,' she told Janet. 'I'm going to give Jonathan a call.'

'It's still too early,' Janet groaned. 'Can't you stop it again?'

'Not this time.' Fiona squeezed her hand. 'Don't worry. We've done well getting this far.'

Janet tried to smile. 'I haven't finished the scrapbook yet. I could do with another week or two.'

'I'm surprised it's lasted this long,' was Jonathan's reaction when Fiona beeped him. 'We'll have to move fast and remove the suture. We don't want to risk a uterine rupture. How many weeks is she now?'

'Almost twenty-eight,' Fiona replied. 'She's been in for four weeks now.'

'Still early, but we can be a lot more optimistic about the outcome,' Jonathan said. 'Especially with the new lot of steroids on board. Can I leave it to you to contact Theatre and Paediatrics? I'll help Martin until you're ready for me.'

'Of course.' Fiona felt relieved at the prospect of directing her energies towards a particular goal. She was drained personally by the family crisis and, to a lesser extent, by her own problems. She wasn't able to formulate a specific goal for herself yet, so energy spent in that direction seemed formless and wasted.

Focusing on Janet Redbury gave her the bubble of professional enthusiasm she had begun to fear she'd lost. Determined to succeed, her step became purposeful and her eyes brightened as she made the preparations.

With the suture removed, labour progressed quickly and naturally. Jonathan let Fiona do the delivery herself. It was the first time she had delivered such a premature baby, and Fiona had to use every ounce of her skill to protect the tiny infant. She was grateful to have Doreen Roberts with her team on hand to take over, and was rewarded by Doreen's compliment on her handling of the delivery. The baby girl was small but healthy, and Doreen seemed confident.

'The growth rate over the last few weeks has been excellent, and with the booster course of steroids Janet's just had we're in a far better position than we would have been. All round, I'd say the treatment has been very successful.'

Janet Redbury and her husband, watching as their

daughter was transferred into an incubator, echoed their agreement.

'You made it possible for us to get this far,' Janet told Fiona emotionally. 'You don't know how much it means to us.'

Fiona's hand moved under her white coat, her fingertips just brushing her own abdomen. 'I think I do.' she said smilingly.

'Just as well it was a girl,' Janet laughed.

Fiona nodded. 'Daisy would be a rotten name for a boy.'

Doreen lagged behind her registrar and caught Jonathan's eye as Fiona was talking to the Redburys. She spoke quietly but her words carried as Fiona finished speaking.

'How about dinner tonight, Jon? I've got a fantastic piece of venison in my fridge.'

'No, thanks, Doreen. I'm rather tied up.'

Fiona busied herself, taking Janet's blood pressure, but her heart was racing. She delayed putting the stethoscope ear pieces in place as Doreen spoke again.

'Another night, then?' Her tone was confident.

'I don't think so.'

Fiona had to bite back a smile. She didn't dare risk a glance at Doreen to see how she was reacting to the polite but meaningful rebuff she had received.

'Actually,' Jonathan said carefully, 'I'm vegetarian.'

Martin was seeing the final outpatient of the day when Fiona made it back downstairs. She passed various staff members, cleaning up the department and complaining about their feet. She made her way to the ultrasound room at the end of the corridor. Lisa, too, was sorting out her equipment and packing up for the day. Fiona slipped into the room and closed the door behind her.

'Would you mind an extra patient?'

Lisa groaned. 'I'm all finished. Martin's taking me out for dinner.' She smiled shyly. 'We're celebrating.' Lisa held out her left hand to show Fiona the ring.

'Wow! Congratulations.' Fiona grinned with genuine pleasure. 'You guys haven't wasted any time.'

'Well, when you know it's the right person there isn't any doubt, is there? Or if there is I suppose it's not the right person.'

'I'm sure you're right,' Fiona agreed. Had she ever had any doubt who the right person was for her? She thought she had. He had sown the seed himself. It was up to her whether she let it germinate, however. Finally she seemed to be facing a choice she was allowed to make on her own. It was one she considered herself to be still postponing. She smiled again at Lisa.

'I know you'll both be very happy. I won't hold you up.'

'Who's the patient, anyway?

'Me.' Fiona had to laugh at Lisa's shocked expression. 'It's OK. I was a bit shocked myself at first, but I'm very happy about it now. I'd rather nobody else knew just yet, though.'

Lisa glanced at the door and then went over to lock it. 'Come on, then. We've got a few minutes before Martin will be finished.'

Fiona climbed up onto the bed. 'Thanks, Lisa.' She rolled down the top of her leggings, exposing her still flat stomach.

'Did you hear that Jack Owens has definitely resigned?' Lisa was turning her machine back on and adjusting the controls.

'No, I didn't. Martin will be pleased—he's got a good chance of getting the consultancy here.'

'I don't know about that.' Lisa eyed Fiona speculatively as she reached for the tube of gel. 'When he was talking to Jon Fletcher about it, he said that there may be a job for him in Wales sooner than he thinks. For Jack Owens, that is.'

'What did he mean?' Fiona watched the screen flicker into life as Lisa placed the transducer on Fiona's abdomen.

'I gather Mr Fletcher doesn't intend to go back to Wales,' Lisa replied. 'At least, that's what Martin thought he meant. He's a bit worried. If Jon decided he wanted to stay here the competition would be too stiff for us.' Lisa sighed, but then brightened. 'Anyway, let's see what we can find here.'

'It's a bit early for a scan,' Fiona admitted, allowing herself to be distracted from the gossip. 'But there's something I'd really like to check out.'

By mid-week Matthew Donaldson had been moved from CCU into the cardiology ward, and was starting a rapid mobilisation and rehabilitation programme. With the emergency over, Fiona felt able to voice her own immediate concerns as the family gathered for dinner on Wednesday night.

'Dad's really fretting about the farm,' she began. 'It's not going to help his recovery, being so anxious about the lambing.'

Ruth agreed. 'The Taylors are doing their best, but they've got their own farm to manage as well.'

Alan nodded vigorously. 'It's all arranged. I've got cover for my lecture schedule, and I'm going to drive down this weekend.'

Daniel passed Fiona a bowl of salad. 'I've suggested we hire a manager to help Alan until everything's sorted out. There'll be some good local people available. I'd love to go down myself, but I'll have to get back to Auckland tomorrow. Now that Dad's out of the woods, I can't be away from work any longer. Besides, I'm rather missing Shelley.'

'I miss Belle,' Fiona put in quietly, almost to herself.

'She'll be fine,' Alan assured her. 'She was a farm dog for a long time before she moved into pampered retirement.'

'Gwen will be looking after her,' Ruth added soothingly. 'Don't worry.'

'She'll still feel deserted,' Fiona insisted. Looking up, she caught Jonathan's eye. He smiled and Fiona returned the smile gratefully. At least someone understood.

Fiona had arrived at work on Thursday morning, only to be sent home again by Jonathan.

'We're flying down to Queenstown at 10 o'clock,' he'd informed her. 'I've arranged everything. Go and pack enough for a few days.'

Fiona had shaken her head in protest, but Jonathan stood firm.

'I've got to return all the equipment we borrowed from the hospital, and Belle needs collecting, don't you think?'

Fiona had nodded then with a smile.

'I could do it on my own, but I thought you could

help check out the farm before Alan gets there. That way, you can ring your dad to stop him fretting.'

Fiona had nodded again with enthusiasm. 'I need my car, too. But you could have driven that back.'

'I could.' Jonathan had given Fiona a direct look. 'But I think you could do with a break. The last one didn't work out so well, did it?'

'No.' Fiona's smile had become a chuckle.

'And maybe it's time we had a talk,' Jonathan had added quietly. 'I couldn't think of a better place than home, could you?'

As the plane descended through the amazingly clear skies over the lake, which reflected the intense blue, and below the level of the still snow-capped craggy peaks of the Remarkables, Fiona had to agree that Jonathan was right. If ever there was a place to sort things out and find peace then this was it.

They rented a car at the airport, loading it with all the equipment they were returning to the hospital. It would have been a quick detour to drop it off on their way to the farm but Fiona, now so close, was desperately keen to reassure herself that all was well at home—in particular that Belle was all right.

The talk as they followed the road around the lake was practical and impersonal but quite relaxed. They both knew they now had the time and their own space to work in. Fiona had the feeling that Jonathan was waiting for her to initiate any discussion, that he was being careful not to put any pressure on her.

The feeling intensified after they had spoken to the Taylors and had accepted the quick lunch they were offered. Jonathan stayed at the homestead only long enough to watch the joyous reunion between Fiona and Belle, before leaving to go back to the district hospital. Fiona stayed in the house for some time after he left. She consulted the list Ruth had given her, packing a suitcase with all the small necessities they were missing, especially Matthew's reading glasses and Ruth's needlepoint project.

She tidied and cleaned the kitchen, feeling a pang as she remembered the horror of her father's collapse. His partly eaten lunch was still on the table. Gwen had apologised for not being able to do anything in the house, but the police had kept the keys. What with lambing season gearing up to full swing, they were all flat out on the farm, in any case.

Fiona wondered about Jonathan's lengthy absence, but decided that he'd probably been invited for a beer with the hospital staff. She cleaned out and stoked the coal range, grateful for the warmth that began to radiate almost instantly. It was going to be a cold night—perhaps the last frost of the season, judging by the crisp feel to the air as the afternoon light began to fade.

Fiona took some of her mother's soup and bread from the freezer and put it on top of the coal range to thaw, then she found her anorak and some warm gloves. She and Jonathan had planned to take the farm bikes out that afternoon to check the sheep, but Fiona knew there was not enough daylight left now. The best she could do was to check the home paddock herself. The rest would have to wait until tomorrow.

Fiona skirted the stables and outbuildings, climbed a stile and watched Belle squeeze through the wires of the fence, before setting off up the sloping paddock that led to a stand of pine trees. The sheep were congregating there for shelter and Fiona could see already that there were quite a few new arrivals. It was a large paddock, and Fiona had to slow her pace as she became out of breath. She didn't notice the figure well behind her, negotiating the stile.

Belle trotted by her side, ignoring the sheep around her. Being of a dignified age, chasing the brainless balls of wool had now lost its attraction. As they neared the top end of the paddock, however, Belle stopped and barked, drawing Fiona's attention to one recumbent sheep. The ground around the animal was well churned up and it had clearly been in distress for some time. The reason was obvious. A front leg and the face of a lamb protruded from the ewe, the birthing process having stalled completely. The lamb looked dead.

'Oh, hell!' Fiona scrambled to help the sheep, but the ewe made a frantic effort to rise and trotted away further up the hill. Fiona followed.

'Hold her, Belle,' she commanded.

Belle sneaked in behind the sheep and stood with lowered head—a picture of alertness. Retired she might be, but the skills were there when needed.

Fiona stood on the other side of the ewe and pondered her next move. The trees and the fence were on one side, but the ewe could break free and run downhill if she panicked and got past Belle. A high-speed run was the last thing either Fiona or the ewe needed. Suddenly the gap was filled by Jonathan. Fiona's surprise and relief showed in her exclamation as she saw Jonathan grin and give her a thumbs-up signal.

The three moved together to corner the ewe. With an expert lunge, Jonathan caught the animal and drew a leg up to force it down. He held the head firmly and nodded at Fiona.

'See what you can do, Pen. Unless you want this end?'

'No, thanks.' Fiona stripped off her gloves. 'I'd rather have the interesting bit.'

Without much hope, Fiona worked to extract the lamb. She had to push the head back inside to find and free the trapped foreleg. Then it required some effort to pull the lamb out. The mother was too exhausted to help push and now lay immobile, even though Jonathan had released his hold. Fiona laid the limp form of the lamb to one side.

'Not much hope there.'

'Hang on—don't give up that easily.' Jonathan grabbed a handful of pine needles from the ground and began to rub the lamb. At the same time he opened the tiny mouth to clear it. Fiona turned her attention to the mother, but that, too, seemed hopeless. The final effort of eluding her helpers had been too much, and she was rapidly giving up the struggle.

Jonathan held the lamb to the ewe's teat and squeezed some milk into its mouth. Amazingly the lamb showed some response, and the twitching movements grew stronger as Jonathan continued his rubbing. Belle watched with interest as the lamb latched on and began sucking.

'How's the ewe?' Jonathan asked.

'Nearly gone,' Fiona replied quietly. 'There's nothing we can do for her. We'll be lucky if this is the only loss like this without Dad's vigilance.'

'At least this little chap's had some colostrum.' Jonathan tucked the lamb inside the warm bush shirt he was wearing. 'One for the box, I guess.' He smiled. 'Another Ivan, do you think?'

Fiona's smile was cautious. 'You can't just turn the clock back, Jonathan. It's not that easy.'

'I know.' Jonathan's smile had faded. 'But you can start again sometimes.'

'Sometimes,' Fiona agreed. 'But I thought you'd had enough of wiping the slate clean and starting again.'

'Perhaps I have,' Jonathan said quietly. 'Maybe this time I need to keep what was good and learn from the rest. I think what was good would be a great base to build on.' He took a deep breath. 'Do you think so, Pen?'

Fiona was silent for a long moment. She knew she could bypass the reference to their relationship, and the change of subject would be accepted. But she also knew she didn't want to. She had postponed long enough.

She spoke softly. 'Yes. I think it would be an ideal base to build on.' She moved close to Jonathan and stroked the lamb snuggled inside his shirt. Then she took his hand. 'Come on, we'd better get Ivan the Second, here, into the box. It's nearly dark and getting pretty cold. Also, I'm indescribably filthy.'

Holding hands, they negotiated the hill with some difficulty as dusk overtook them. Their stumbling progress in the dark, coupled with the occasional protest in the form of a wobbly bleat from Ivan, caused more than a little hilarity. By the time they made it back to the homestead they both realised they felt totally at ease in each other's company again. The warmth of the kitchen and the smell of the bubbling soup was a perfect welcome. Fiona went to have a shower while

Jonathan settled the lamb into the box beside the range.

The frosty night had closed in around the isolated house by the time Fiona and Jonathan ate their dinner. They drew their kitchen chairs up close to the range, breaking chunks off the hot loaf of bread to dip into their mugs of soup. For a while they simply ate in a companionable silence. Then Ivan popped his head up over the edge of the large box, bleating loudly. His condition had obviously improved considerably. Fiona and Jonathan laughed and then their gazes caught and held.

'I love you, Pen.'

'I know.' Fiona's smile was shy. 'I love you too, Jon.'

'I haven't said this properly because I didn't think you would hear me. I'm sorry.'

Fiona dropped her gaze to the mug in her hands.

'I want you to know how much I regret my mistakes.'

Fiona's smile and glance were fleeting. 'You mean there was more than one?'

Jonathan returned her smile with his one-sided version. 'A countless number, I imagine, but there's two I'm thinking of. First, doubting your word about the baby—or, rather, for doubting the value you placed on our relationship and making the crass assumption that you might have gone straight from me to someone else.'

'Definitely crass,' Fiona agreed. 'But, given your history and looking at it from your point of view, I guess it's forgivable.'

Jonathan placed his soup mug on top of the range.

'Perhaps an even bigger mistake I made was to ignore the importance of what we had between us. I thought I was doing the right thing by you in putting the brakes on our relationship. I had no right to make that choice for you, and in doing so I created the biggest emotional mess I've ever been in. What was worse was that I had also created it for you.'

'I did my own share of doubting and creating, you know,' Fiona said firmly. 'I'll forgive you if you forgive me.'

'Done.'

'Mind you, I might not be so accommodating next time.'

'There won't be a next time,' Jonathan promised. 'I'll never doubt you or me or us again. Ever.'

'So, are you going to make a respectable woman of me, then?'

'Of course. But give me time to find a ring and think of the most romantic place possible for a proposal. I'd like to do it properly. Perfectly, in fact.'

'OK.' Fiona grinned contentedly. 'Would you like some more soup?'

'Yes, please.' Jonathan held out his mug and Fiona filled it again. They drew their chairs closer so that their bodies touched as they finished their meal. Belle shuffled nearer and lay on their feet.

'Where and when, do you think?' Jonathan asked.

'Here, of course. It's home.' Fiona knew he was referring to their wedding. 'And let's do it at Christmas. That way we'll always have a huge family celebration on our anniversary.'

Jonathan nodded. 'And by then I should know whether anything's come from my visit this afternoon.'

'What do you mean?'

'I've decided to apply for a job at the hospital here. Do you think you could be happy out of the big smoke?'

'Of course. But could you?'

Jonathan leaned over and kissed Fiona's lips gently once, then again. 'I don't think I could feel happy anywhere else. This is where you and I belong. It's home.'

'Sounds perfect to me.' Fiona set her mug down carefully. 'And there's always general practice—if I'm not too busy with parenthood, that is.'

'Speaking of which I never thought I could be a father so you know I'm thrilled beyond words about the baby, but…' Jonathan frowned slightly '…this little miracle is rather unlikely to happen again. I remember you said you wanted six kids.'

Fiona bit her lip. 'I also said I'd be happy with two.'

Jonathan's mouth gaped. 'You don't mean—'

'I had a scan this week,' Fiona said demurely. 'Far be it from me to fly in the face of family tradition.'

Ivan's head shot up over the edge of the box again. His bleat was now positively raucous. Laughing, Jonathan folded Fiona into his arms and kissed her again, this time very firmly.

'Sounds perfect to me.'